THE MAN OF HER DREAMS

MARCIA LYNN McCLURE

Published by Distractions Ink
P.O. Box 15971
Rio Rancho, NM 87174

Published by Distractions Ink
©Copyright 2013 by M. Meyers
A.K.A. Marcia Lynn McClure
Cover Photography by ©Monkey Business
Images/Dreamstime.com and ©M. Meyers
Cover Design and Interior Graphics by
Sandy Ann Allred/Timeless Allure

First Printed Edition: December 2013

McClure, Marcia Lynn, 1965—
The Man of Her Dreams: a novella/by Marcia Lynn McClure.

ISBN: 978-0-9913878-0-9
Library of Congress Control Number: 2013958412

Printed in the United States of America

To Shannon,
My totally awesome fellow '80s chick!
Thank you for so many, many things
(including turkey turds)
But especially for such warm, supportive,
and comfortable friendship!
You are, in essence, a protector of my soul.

CHAPTER ONE

Libby Meadows yawned as she drowsily descended the stairs from her cozy attic room. Pausing for a moment as she reached the bottom floor, she inhaled, relishing the blended scents of bolts of new fabric and cinnamon.

It was a little cool in the quilt shop—a sure sign that autumn had indeed settled in. But Libby didn't mind. She liked the modest chill of fall mornings—found them invigorating, not to mention a perfect excuse to have hot chocolate available for customers. And customers always bought more fabric when they'd been warmed inside by a nice, steaming mug of hot cocoa.

Not that Libby was all about sales and money, but she did have to worry about it to some regard. After all, she'd inherited the quilt shop from her Grandma Hannah when her grandmother had passed away the year before, and Libby was determined to keep the quilt shop open and thriving. Therefore, she did have to think about pleasing her customers, and hot cocoa on a brisk autumn morning would certainly do the trick.

As she walked down the shop aisle displaying the bolts and bolts of gold, orange, and crimson autumn prints, Libby couldn't help but reach out, allowing her fingers to trail over the fresh cotton lined up so perfectly on the shelf. She loved the feel of cotton fabric, loved the fragrance of it when it was being ironed, loved the colors and the works of art that could be created from it.

Libby paused when she heard a key wiggling in the front doorknob of the old Victorian house that had long ago been converted into a quilt shop. Peering around the corner of a large fabric case, she smiled as Sue O'Shannon stepped into the shop and began fumbling with the keypad that disabled the alarm system.

"Good morning," Libby greeted as Sue at last punched in the correct code to disengage the alarm.

"That thing makes me so nervous, Libby!" Sue exclaimed, shaking her head as she plopped her purse onto the register counter by the front door. "I'm always afraid I'm going to punch in the wrong code, and then before we know it, the cops will be racing down here and thinking I'm an idiot because I set the alarm off."

Libby laughed. "Well, if you weren't so prompt—even early most of the time—I'd have it turned off, and you wouldn't have to worry about it."

"No, no," Sue insisted, however. "It's good for me. It teaches me to focus…you know, in case I ever have to defuse a bomb or something."

"Oh yeah, that's what I always equate it to as well," Libby said, smiling as she watched her friend and employee hang her jacket on the coatrack behind the door.

"It's gorgeous out there this morning!" Sue exclaimed then. "The air…it's just rich with the scent of leaves, and someone is burning pine in their fireplace somewhere close. It's heavenly!"

Libby sighed with satisfaction. "We better get the hot chocolate going then," she said. "This kind of weather always brings people into the shop." Her smile faded a bit. "Though it's days like this that I wish we could just close up and wander along the river, you know?"

"I *do* know," Sue admitted. She shrugged, however. "But we get a shipment today, and that always makes the work more enjoyable." As Sue started toward the back of the shop to where a small kitchen was located, she called, "Do you want the instant hot cocoa today? Or do you want to pop for your good stuff?"

"Let's pop for the good stuff," Libby answered. "I feel like really enjoying every moment today. Maybe I'll even get Mrs. Blair's quilt finished. I know how badly she wants to get it to her new great-grandbaby."

"I doubt you'll have too much time for quilting in the back room today," Sue said, however. "I bet we'll be hopping with sales."

"I hope so," Libby admitted. It was a worry— running one's own business—especially in a down economy. "Oh!" she exclaimed as she remembered something. "I forgot to mention that the contractor my dad hired to do our sewing room is coming today to take measurements and stuff. So if I'm not here, just show him where we want the sewing room and machine stations and things, okay?"

"Of course," Sue assured Libby. "It's so great that your dad found a contractor for you. You certainly don't have time to shuffle through bids this time of year. We'll be kicking from now until December twenty-third. Do you think the guy can have the sewing room done in time for us to begin holding classes in January?"

Libby nodded. "Oh yeah. He told Dad it would only take him about three weeks start to finish."

"Wow, really?" Sue called from the kitchen. "But you still want to wait to start classes until January, right?"

"Absolutely! I don't think I could handle one more thing right now," Libby admitted. "I've got more quilting orders coming in than I expected, so you really will have to do quite a bit of quilting for me too, okay?"

"No problem," Sue called. "I'm just wondering where you're going to find the time to work on your own projects this year."

But Libby smiled to herself as she thought of the fairy house she was constructing for Sue. "Oh, don't worry. I'll steal time here and there."

Libby couldn't wait to give Sue the fairy house she'd been working on for her. She'd put a ton of thought into what to construct the whimsical house out of, not to mention the décor. In fact, Libby had once spent two hours in the local antique shop looking for just the right teacup to serve as the fairy's bathtub in Sue's fairy house. Finally, she'd chosen a pretty three-footed china teacup with a colorful pastoral scene on it. Sue's fairy house was turning out to be a little larger than Libby had originally planned to make it. Nevertheless, it was already so beautiful that Libby wondered how she was going to part with it when it was finished and the time came to give it to Sue for Christmas.

Snapping her fingers as she remembered that she'd wanted to search for a few acorn hats to put in the fairy house cupboards to serve as bowls, Libby said, "Oh! I've got to remember to do that!"

"To do what?" Sue called from the kitchen.

"Oh, just something I keep forgetting to do," Libby answered.

"How much vanilla extract do you want me to leave out?" Sue asked.

"One of those little glass bottles should do it. It only releases a couple of drops at a time, so that way it's just perfect," Libby said.

At that moment, Libby heard the familiar tinkle of the old bell hanging just inside the door skip through the room.

Glancing over, she saw Mrs. Blair step into the store.

"Well, goodness' sakes, Mrs. Blair!" Libby exclaimed, smiling. "You're in awful early this morning! And I was just telling Sue that I'm going to try and finish quilting that quilt for your new great-grandson today."

Mrs. Blair smiled at Libby, tipping her head down to look at her over the top of her glasses.

"Well, don't you look perky and pretty this morning, Libby Meadows," Mrs. Blair greeted.

"Well, thank you," Libby said.

Libby loved the sound of Mrs. Blair's voice. It was light and airy. Mrs. Blair was tall, with teased and shaped white hair that looked just like she had a big snowball piled on top of her head. Furthermore, she always wore clothes that reminded Libby of a bright wintry day—sky blue, white, silver—and they became her perfectly.

"I've just come in for some fat quarters, dear," Mrs. Blair said. "I'm working on one of my I Spy quilts, and I need some jungle prints…and maybe some chickens, if you have them."

"And if I don't have them already cut, I'll cut them for you," Libby offered.

Walking to the juvenile section, Libby retrieved the basket of fat quarters from one shelf near the jungle-themed fabrics.

"I've got monkeys…lions…oh! Here's one with tons of animals," she said, offering one of the folded fat quarters to Mrs. Blair.

"Oh, perfect! I love that one!" Mrs. Blair exclaimed as her dark, wintry-blue eyes sparkled with pleasure. Taking the basket of fat quarters from Libby, she said, "I'll just browse awhile, dear. You go on about your business. I don't want to keep you from anything."

Libby nodded, amused by the way Mrs. Blair always became so instantly engrossed in searching for just the right fabrics. One would've thought the world around her had come to a halt.

"Would you like some hot chocolate this morning?" Libby offered. "It's my own recipe today."

"Mmm hmmm…as soon as I've found what I'm looking for, dear," Mrs. Blair mumbled, her attention rapt on the contents of the basket she held.

Libby giggled a little. "Okay, well, you just let me know if you need anything."

"Of course, dear," Mrs. Blair mumbled again.

Again the soft ring-a-ling of the front door bell tumbled into the room.

"Good morning," Libby greeted with a smile as a group of four women entered the shop. "Can I help you ladies with something?"

All four women smiled, and one of them answered, "Not yet. But I'm sure we'll need a ton of stuff cut eventually."

Libby smiled. She recognized the women as having come in the week before. They were all new to the growing resurgence of quilting as a hobby and had dropped several hundred dollars each when they'd been in previously. They'd also signed up to begin taking quilting classes in January.

Therefore, though she hadn't memorized each of their names yet, Libby was determined that she'd have them down pat by the time she'd cut whatever lengths of fabric tempted them that day.

"Sue has the fixings for homemade hot chocolate back there in the kitchen if you ladies would like to enjoy a mug while you browse," Libby tempted.

"Ooo! Homemade hot chocolate?" one of the ladies asked with obvious interest.

"You mean with milk instead of water?" another asked as her eyes widened with anticipation.

Libby nodded. "Well, kind of. I use sugar, cocoa, a bit of vanilla, a little water, and evaporated milk. It's how my mom always makes it, and I love it! I even have some flavored creamers if you'd like to add it in. I prefer amaretto myself. But believe me, my hot chocolate is rich enough on its own."

"I'm sold!" the fourth woman exclaimed. "Where is it, and how much for a mug?"

Libby giggled, pointed toward the kitchen, and answered, "Right back there in our kitchen...and it's complimentary."

"I'm in!" one of the other women giggled.

"Me too!" another woman added.

With a nod of approval in Libby's direction, the fourth woman followed her friends toward the kitchen.

Libby sighed with delight and satisfaction. Her mom's recipe for hot chocolate never failed to please anyone with either a sweet tooth or a passion for hot chocolate, and it made her happy that it did. Oh sure, it was good for business, but mostly Libby just liked to make people feel warm and happy inside. She figured if the bolts of gorgeous cotton fabric didn't do the trick, a soothing mug of her mom's hot chocolate would.

She heard Sue cheerily greet the ladies as they entered the kitchen and knew the customers were in good hands. Sue was so good with people—so cheerful and kind—not to mention an incredible quilter with a ton of knowledge. Libby knew she was blessed in far too many ways to list by having Sue O'Shannon as a friend.

Libby heard the bell ting-a-ling again. She quickly glanced to Mrs. Blair, ensuring that the older woman was still engrossed in finding just the perfect fat quarters for her current quilt project, before looking toward the door to greet another customer.

"Holy cow!" Libby exclaimed in a whisper as she saw that a man had just entered the shop—a tall, broad-shouldered man with the bluest eyes Libby had ever seen, the most perfectly squared jaw she'd ever seen, the straightest nose she'd ever seen, the strongest cheekbones she'd ever seen, and brown hair that begged to have female fingers run through it. The overpoweringly handsome young man wore work boots that looked they'd been through a war, well-worn jeans, a blue and black flannel shirt, and a tool belt.

"Good morning," Libby greeted, figuring the guy had to be the contractor her father had hired to create her sewing room. Why else would a good-looking slice of eye candy, complete with a tool belt, be visiting the shop?

"Hi," the man responded, smiling as he strode toward her. "I'm Sawyer Delaney," he said, offering a hand. Libby smiled in return and accepted his warm, strong handshake. "I'm the guy who's going to do the remodel in here. Are you the owner?"

"Yeah," Libby said, nodding. "I'm Libby…Libby Meadows."

"Nice to meet you," the man said. He paused for a moment, grinning at her as if he knew something she didn't. Then, once her blush really begun to heat up her cheeks, he said, "So…I understand you're needing a space where ladies can come to have lessons and things? Right?"

Libby nodded. "Yeah. I'm going to start holding classes after the first of the year, and that back room I'm going to use is hideous…and really, really cold in the winter too."

Sawyer Delaney's smile broadened. "Well, let's see what I can do for you then," he said. "Just show me where this hideous, cold room is, and I'll get started. I'll get some measurements and work up a couple of options for you, and then we can settle on colors and anything else that needs nailing down, okay?"

"Okay," Libby agreed.

She felt strange—sort of unsettled in her stomach and lightheaded for a moment. She made a mental note that she really needed to start including more protein in her breakfast. The granola bar she'd snatched from the drawer in her nightstand just wasn't doing the trick—or so she assumed by the strange sensation washing over her.

"Sue?" she called.

"Yeah?" Sue responded, peering out from the kitchen. The moment Sue spied the handsome contractor, however, her eyes bugged out like a gerbil trapped in a toddler's fist, and she left the kitchen and hurried toward Libby—or rather, the contractor.

"This is Mr. Delaney," Libby began to explain. "He's here to do the remodel stuff on the sewing instruction area. Will you watch the shop while I show him where everything is?"

"You bet," Sue agreed, blushing a bit as she gazed at Sawyer Delaney a moment.

"Thanks." Looking to the drop-dead gorgeous contractor her father had found to handle the remodel project, she said, "If you just wanna follow me…it's right back here."

"Of course," the man agreed.

As Libby led Sawyer toward the back room that would serve as the sewing instruction area, he commented, "This is a great shop you have. It's got a real charm, you know? All cozy and inviting. It smells good too."

"Thanks," Libby giggled, "though you seem a bit surprised on the smells good part."

Sawyer laughed. "Well, in truth, it *is* kind of a surprise. Most of these old houses smell kind of musty, you know? Even if they've been renovated. But not yours. Yours smells sort of like my grandma's kitchen did when I was kid."

Libby sighed with being pleased. "Good! Hearing that makes me happy, 'cause that's what I'm going for—grandma's kitchen. I want customers to want to linger, you know? Feel soothed and tranquil, take their time browsing, and enjoy themselves."

"So they'll want to come back," Sawyer offered with an obviously keen business insight.

"Yeah," Libby admitted. "But I also just want them to escape the noise and chaos outside the shop for a while. Know what I mean?"

"I do," he answered, to her delight added, "and if a guy's opinion means anything, you've definitely got the ambiance going in here," he assured her.

"Thanks!" she giggled. "And a guy's opinion means a lot, because if you feel that way—like you're in your grandma's house—then I'm sure women will. Oh! And don't forget to have some hot chocolate before you leave today. It's my mom's recipe, and you'll never be able to fully enjoy the instant stuff again."

"Homemade hot chocolate, huh?" He smiled. "Wow, you really do know how to draw people in."

"I hope so," Libby sighed. "My grandma started this shop when I was a little girl, and I'm determined to keep it the success it was when she was here."

"Your dad said his mom left the shop and house to you when she passed away?" he ventured.

"Yep. And it's hard to keep a retail business alive in this economy," Libby admitted. "That's why, when people started asking me if I'd be willing to teach sewing and quilting, well, I thought it might be a good idea to hop on that demand right away. Grandma left some money for the business, and I really think putting in a sewing and quilting area will be worth the cost in the end."

Libby stepped into the back room that was going to be the sewing area. "I want to keep the old fireplace for sure," she began. She glanced up into Sawyer's handsome face and added, "You know, the ambiance it will add during the cold months and all."

"Very wise decision," he agreed.

Libby sighed. "I'm guessing Dad gave you a pretty good outline already. I need, like, six sewing stations, and I'd like to have some cupboards and…well, I'm sure you already have all that down."

"I do," Sawyer admitted. "So I'll just start by taking some measurements. And your dad said the electrical and plumbing have already been updated?"

"Yeah. Grandma had that done a couple of years before she passed away," Libby explained. "Almost like she knew…"

Sawyer smiled with understanding as Libby's voice trailed off.

"Like she was preparing it for you ahead of time, hmmm?" he offered.

"Yeah."

"And your dad says you live here, in an attic room," Sawyer commented. He chuckled a little, and the low rumble of his masculine amusement made Libby's heart leap with admiration. "That's even more charming than the atmosphere in the shop—the quilting girl in the attic room. I really like attic bedrooms. They have tons more character than regular bedrooms, you know?"

"I do," Libby agreed.

"Well, I see that you've already got customers this morning, so you don't have to worry about babysitting me," he began. "I'll get my initial measurements and then run by tomorrow with some designs for you to choose from, all right?"

"All right," Libby answered, disturbed at how elated she'd felt when he said he'd be in the next day. "I'll leave you to your work then. But don't forget to stop in at the kitchen and have some hot chocolate before you leave, okay?"

"Will do. Thanks," he said.

Libby bit her lip, delighted as he winked at her before she turned to leave. Holy smokes, he was handsome! Like, criminally handsome! It certainly wouldn't be a chore to have Sawyer Delaney in and out of the quilt shop every day for a few weeks.

Sawyer grinned as he made his initial visual survey of the room. Don Meadows hadn't mentioned that his daughter was such an eyeful. Somehow Sawyer had immediately thought Libby Meadows would be kind of a plain Jane for some reason. He guessed that finding the quilt shop owner was as pretty as a summer sunrise would teach him not to make assumptions based on the kind of business a person ran.

Still, he gave himself some slack, being that the only quilter he'd ever known before was his grandma. Who would've thought the owner of a quilt shop would be an attractive twenty-something girl?

He liked her brown and blonde highlighted hair—straightened, but incredibly softening to her appearance. He thought he'd noticed her eyes were green...or light brown. Either way, they sparkled when she talked about her grandmother, her shop, or the remodel. He could tell the girl's heart was in the business, along with a lot of hard work.

"Homemade hot chocolate, eh?" he mumbled aloud. Grinning, he added, "Well, Libby Meadows, you sure do know how to keep the female customers coming back." Sawyer chuckled to himself, however. He wasn't even a big hot chocolate fan, but the atmosphere in the quilt shop—the warm lighting, the scents of cinnamon, nutmeg, and apples—all of it was making his mouth water as he wondered what Libby's homemade hot chocolate would taste like.

"Yep. This girl has got a good business sense," Sawyer said as he hunkered down to inspect the old fireplace. "Not to mention one nice little figure."

CHAPTER TWO

"Wow! What did your dad do? Run out and find the hottest contractor for you that he could?" Sue asked in a whisper when Libby returned to the front room of the shop.

Libby giggled, "One might think that, right? He's a dream! Like, seriously!"

"I know!" Sue agreed. "And how long is he supposed to be here? Three weeks? We'll be too distracted every time he walks through, and we won't get anything done!"

"Well, he must work as good as he looks," Libby began. "This is, like, the fourth job Dad has given him."

"This hot chocolate is to die for!" one of the four ladies who had arrived in the shop just prior to Sawyer chimed. "Do you mind sharing the recipe?"

Libby smiled. "Of course not. In fact..." Reaching toward a little basket she kept clipped to one side of the fabric-cutting counter, she retrieved a small card. "Here you go. I had these printed up a while back...because so many customers kept asking for the recipe."

The woman smiled, accepted the card Libby offered, and tucked it inside the outer pocket on her purse. "Thanks so much! I'm Jennie," she said. "I signed up for one of your classes when I was in last week."

"I remember! I think you'll really like the class. And, officially, I'm Libby, by the way," Libby said.

"You own the shop, right?" Jennie asked.

"Mmm hmmm. It was my grandmother's, and when she passed away, it came to me," Libby explained.

"Well, I love it!" Jennie exclaimed, looking around at the bolts of fabric that lined the shelves on every wall.

"Me too," another one of the women said as she exited the kitchen and strode toward them. "I'm Alisa. When Jennie brought us in last week, I had no idea how great your shop would be…but it's wonderful! I love it! And the hot chocolate will certainly keep me coming back. I'm excited for the classes to start as well."

"Oh, I'm so glad to hear that," Libby offered, smiling, but feeling really nervous internally. She hoped the classes would be worth the money the ladies who were all signing up would pay.

The other two women appeared then, both gently blowing over the tops of steaming mugs full of hot cocoa.

"I'm Sarah," one of the women said.

"And I'm Kristina," the fourth woman said. "And seriously, this shop is incredible. I wasn't all that into the idea of learning to quilt until Jennie brought us in last week. Now I'm totally excited!"

"Oh, I'm so happy to hear that," Libby giggled.

"And…um…does the hot contractor come as a bonus amenity to the quilting lessons?" Sarah whispered. All four women quietly giggled.

"I'm afraid not," Libby answered. "Though it would be nice, wouldn't it? Just to have something to look at?"

"Yes, it would!" Kristina agreed. "I think I'd sign up for double lessons if that guy were going to be hanging around the shop all the time."

"Hmmm…maybe we could keep breaking things or something to keep him coming back in once in a while," Sue teased. "I'm Sue, by the way. And I'll actually be teaching the class you guys signed up for."

"Awesome!" Jennie exclaimed. "So you're the one we talk to about getting Libby's contractor back for special appearances?"

"That would be me," Sue giggled.

"And even if we can't coax him back for you ladies, if you come in over the next couple of months, we'll not only have hot chocolate readily available but treats too," Libby interjected. She figured it was best to change the subject from the hot contractor that was only temporary to something to entice the customers to come back on a regular basis—food!

"Ooo! Treats!" Alisa cooed. "What kind?"

"Well, we do mostly pumpkin treats in October, starting next week," Libby answered.

"But in November, Libby makes the best turkey turds and brings them in almost every day," Sue explained with enthusiasm.

Four sets of curious, rather doubtful eyebrows rose as the women looked at Sue.

"Turkey turds?" Sarah asked.

"Um, well, I think we might start calling them turkey ploops for the customers that aren't familiar with them yet," Libby explained.

"But they're really called turkey turds, and they are delicious!" Sue assured the women. "Of course, they don't taste like real turkey turds; they just look like them. They're sort of these caramel, maple-flavored puffed corn things Libby makes and—"

"I'm in!" Kristina announced. "I don't care what they're called. If it's caramel, I'm in!"

"Me too," Jennie giggled.

"Pardon me, ladies," Sawyer said, appearing from behind one of the bolt shelves then. "But may I speak with you again for just a minute, Libby?"

"He could speak to me for a lot longer than a minute...like, for the rest of my life," Sarah mumbled into her hot cocoa mug.

"Amen, sister," Alisa mumbled into hers.

"Of course," Libby answered. She was embarrassed by the blush that rose to her cheeks as he gestured that she should precede him.

Once they were back inside the area to be remodeled, Sawyer began, "I just want to verify that you do want to keep the old wood-burning fireplace. You don't want a gas or electric fireplace installed in its place, right?"

"Right," Libby answered.

Golly! He made her so giggly and unsettled inside. It was simultaneously wonderful and unnerving.

"Okay, then I'm going to give you a card," Sawyer said, pulling a card out from under the clip on his clipboard. "This is a guy I suggest you have come clean your chimney before the burning season next year. I'll have him come out and really give your fireplace a good, thorough cleaning when we begin the renovation, but I would suggest you have him sweep it every year. He's really reasonable, and it's a lot more work than people realize to properly maintain a wood-burning fireplace or stove."

Libby frowned, doubting her decision to keep the original fireplace. "Do you think I shouldn't keep it? Should I put in a gas one?"

But Sawyer smiled a perfectly dazzling smile and said, "Absolutely not! Keep this one. First of all, the masonry is awesome! The mantel...that's good, solid, antique oak. And nothing beats a real-live crackling fire. You know?"

Libby smiled with renewed confidence in her decision. "That's what I think. Thanks for the reassurance."

"Anytime," he said, winking at her.

Libby wondered if Sawyer knew he'd winked at her. Or maybe it was just an unconscious, friendly habit— like her grandpa used to do.

"Anything else?" she prodded.

But Sawyer shook his head. "Nope, not for now. I just didn't want you to have to make that decision while entertaining customers, you know?"

Libby nodded. "Good point."

"I'll be about another forty-five minutes, and then I'll be out for some of that hot chocolate you're tempting everyone with, okay?" he said.

"Okay," she answered. "It's worth it. I promise."

"I'm sure it is," he chuckled.

"Well, I guess I'll just leave you to your...you know, to your whatever you need to do," Libby stammered. "Do come get me if you have any other questions, okay?"

"You bet," Sawyer agreed with another wink.

It was totally weird—the way Libby had to literally force herself to leave him and return to the customers in the shop. She suddenly flashed back to how much fun she and her friends used to have during recess in elementary school, dragging magnets through the sand on the playground to see who could gather the most iron filings. And that's exactly how she felt where Sawyer Delaney was concerned—like he was a big horseshoe magnet and she was made up of a billion iron filings that couldn't resist him.

"Sheesh! He's a complete stranger," Libby mumbled to herself as she hurried back to the shop. It wasn't like the man of her dreams had simply waltzed into the quilt shop, his eyes meeting hers, sending little lightning bolts zinging between their gazes like some dumb cartoon.

Yet even as she tried to convince herself that this Sawyer Delaney, whom she'd known for all of thirty minutes, wouldn't ever play a large role in her life, Libby's heartbeat quickened at the thought of him being in the same building with her.

Libby returned to the front of the shop to find Sue busily cutting fat quarters for Mrs. Blair and the other four customers piling bolt after bolt of pretty cotton on the second half of the cutting table.

"Wow!" Libby exclaimed as she watched the woman named Jennie add three more bolts to the growing pile. "It looks like you guys will have me cutting fabric 'til the cows come home."

Jennie nodded, and Alisa said, "You've got us hooked! What's in that hot chocolate anyway? All of a sudden my mind is reeling with project ideas, and I seem to have lost all self-control."

"That's why you should just bring a wad of cash like me," Sarah said. "Then you know you have just so much to spend."

"Oh, I have cash, all right," Kristina added. "But I've got my debit card too…for when the cash runs out."

Libby giggled with total understanding. There was just something about fabric that made a creative heart beat faster. Every time a new fabric pattern came into the shop, Libby found herself cutting the first yard off the bolt to put in her own collection. It seemed that no matter how many pieces of fabric she had collected over the years, eventually every one found a place in some project—a quilt, a pillowcase, a doll dress. Therefore, even as she was thrilled that the new customers were about to drop a bunch of money, thereby helping pay the bills her grandmother's business generated, she was glad to see the love of fabric spreading to new victims—or rather, kindred spirits.

"And did you find what you were looking for, Mrs. Blair?" Libby asked.

"Mmm hmmm," Mrs. Blair mumbled. "And don't worry about getting my quilt finished today, Libby. I doubt either you or Sue will get a lick of work done while that handsome contractor is in the way."

Libby smiled. "Probably not," she admitted.

Mrs. Blair looked up to Libby and offered a rare smile. "But I will have a cup of that hot chocolate before I go, if that's all right."

"Of course," Libby assured her. "I'll go whip one up for you right now."

"Oh, look at this chicken print!" Libby heard Kristina exclaim. "Is this just too adorable or what? But what would I do with it?"

"Who cares!" Jennie answered. "You'll think of something eventually. Just buy a couple of yards. That's enough for pretty much anything you decide to do."

Again Libby smiled—all too understanding of the excitement that leapt in a woman's chest when she found a fabric print she fell in love with.

♥

"Whew!" Sue puffed as she collapsed into a chair near the cutting table. "I thought those ladies were going to clean us out there for a minute. Do you realize it took us both cutting half an hour to get their fabric cut?"

"I do!" Libby answered, collapsing into the chair next to Sue's.

She sighed with contentment as she gazed out through the large front window of the store and into the beauty of an autumn day. With all the frantic cutting she and Sue had been caught up in, Libby hadn't noticed that the clouds had been gathering in the blue sky. Now there was no blue visible—only the cool silver and gray of rain clouds. Still, Libby didn't mind. She loved the autumn rain. It always seemed more tranquil and lulling than the heavy, thundering monsoon rains of late summer.

A few scarlet maple leaves floated past the window from the ancient maple in the front lawn of the old Victorian house, and Libby smiled.

"It is perfectly picturesque out there right now," she said aloud to Sue. "Just imagine when the remodel is finished and we can have a fire in that old fireplace!" she added with excited anticipation.

"Ooo! I can just smell the woodsmoke now," Sue sighed. "Then we'll be the ones everyone is talking about when they say, 'Someone's got a fire going,' when they're walking through the neighborhood.

"I know, huh?" Libby said, more excited than ever for the renovation to be finished. "I wish I trusted the fireplace up in my room," she commented. "That would be too, too, too dreamy! A fire crackling in the inner hearth—though my grandma always called it a firebox—some soft, romantic music, maybe a glass of cider, some chips, a book..."

"Too dreamy indeed," Sawyer said from the other side of the cutting table, startling both Libby and Sue from their moment of reverie.

"Oh, hi," Libby greeted, turning to face him. "Are you finished for today?"

"I am," he answered. "I'll have a few design options worked up for you by tomorrow afternoon, so I was wondering if you've got some time open that you could fit me in for about thirty minutes. The sooner you make some final decisions on designs, the sooner we can have your instruction area finished."

"Fabulous!" Libby exclaimed. "Um, I can pretty much work around your schedule...so what's good for you?"

"I've got several other client meetings tomorrow," Sawyer said, retrieving his phone from the holster at his belt. "How about…three o'clock?" he asked after having scrolled a bit on his screen.

"That'll be fine," Libby said.

Sawyer smiled. "Great. Now…mind if I try out the hot chocolate those customers were raving about while you two were wielding your rotary cutters?"

Sue and Libby smiled, and as Libby stood up from her chair, Sue said, "It's pretty strong stuff. Hope you have a strong sweet tooth there, Mr. Delaney."

"It has a tendency to relax a person, as well," Libby explained. "Maybe you shouldn't operate any heavy machinery for a while after trying it."

Sawyer chuckled. "Thanks for the warning," he said as he followed Libby to the small kitchen.

Sawyer glanced around the quilt shop's little kitchen. It was in surprisingly good condition. He judged it had been renovated in the mid-1940s by the looks of things.

"This kitchen is in good shape," he commented.

Libby smiled and nodded. "Yeah. My great-grandparents bought this house in the '40s, and my grandma and grandpa purchased it from them in the '60s. Grandma was a great housekeeper, and Grandpa was the best handyman ever…so it has endured very well."

Sawyer grinned, entertained as he watched the little quilt shop owner prepare a large mug of hot chocolate for him. He glanced around again, noting the row of aprons, hanging from a length of wood adorned with old doorknobs. He inhaled deeply the scent of hot chocolate, rich milk, apples, cinnamon, nutmeg, and a number of other spices he recognized but couldn't name.

"I heard you saying something about wishing the attic fireplace were trustworthy?" he ventured.

Libby shrugged. "Yeah. I'd love to have a fire on cold evenings up there. But...well, I have no idea when it was used last...or what kind of shape it's in."

"I'll tell you what," he began. "One day while I'm taking a break from the renovation down here, I'll have a look at it for you...have my fireplace guy check it out and see if it's usable, okay?"

She smiled at him, obviously delighted, and Sawyer was a bit astonished at how the vision warmed his gut.

"Really?" she asked. "I would so, so, so appreciate that. I'll...I'll pay you, of course, and—"

Sawyer shook his head. "Nope. It's not a problem. It won't cost anything to just look at it, okay?"

"Okay. If you're sure," she said, offering him the mug she'd mixed his hot chocolate in.

"I'm sure...and thanks," he assured her, taking the mug.

"Now be careful. Don't burn your tongue," Libby warned him. "And Sue is right. Most men can't handle my hot chocolate. It's rich...more like women prefer."

"So you're saying women like their men *and* their hot chocolate rich, huh?" he teased.

She giggled. "Well, I don't know about the rich men part...but when it comes to chocolate, yes."

Carefully, Sawyer sipped the hot chocolate. It was hot—very hot, the way he preferred. Furthermore, it was, indeed, the richest hot chocolate he'd ever tasted—

nothing like the puny, watered-down stuff available at the concession stands at the local high school football field.

"Wow!" he exclaimed. "You weren't kidding. It's very rich."

"Do you hate it?" Libby asked, her pretty brow puckering with concern.

"Not at all. It's just as good as you claimed…even better," Sawyer answered. "I mean, I couldn't drink a gallon of it; my eyes would be spinning. But it certainly is the best I've ever had."

Libby sighed with relief, her sweet smile returning to her attractive face. "Oh, good. I was afraid you wouldn't like it and then refuse to do the renovation or something."

"No way! I love projects in these old houses," Sawyer explained. "I've never done any kind of renovation on one of these old Victorians that I haven't found something incredible hidden away somewhere."

"Really? Like what?" Libby asked—and Sawyer could see by the sudden spark in her eyes that she was sincerely interested.

He shrugged and answered, "A lot of things. We found an old safe hidden inside a wall we had to remove, and when the new owners of the house were finally able to get it open, it was filled with brand-new Confederate currency—perfectly preserved and totally awesome to see. The ink on the notes wasn't faded. The clerk signatures were as legible as if they'd been signed just the day before. It was pretty incredible."

"Wow! It must've been like finding treasure," Libby offered.

"It was exactly like finding treasure," Sawyer confirmed. He took another sip of the hot chocolate, relishing the way he could feel the warmth travel over his tongue and down the back of his throat all the way to his stomach. Shrugging, he said, "Of course, we don't always find that kind of treasure, but we always find something."

"Well, most of this house has been renovated at one time or another, so I hope it doesn't disappoint you too much when you don't find anything unusual in here," Libby ventured.

"Oh, it won't disappoint me if we don't," Sawyer said. "But we will. There's always something."

Libby smiled as she watched Sawyer drink from the mug of cocoa she'd prepared for him. It was all so exciting—the renovation, the hope of finding something hidden in the house that no one had ever found before, the fact that the handsome contractor would be in and out of her shop and her life for weeks to come. All of a sudden, Libby felt a surge of rejuvenation course through her limbs, for she loved when life brought unexpected pleasures. And seeing the likes of Sawyer Delaney every day certainly would be a pleasure.

CHAPTER THREE

It was downright chilly when Libby awoke the next morning. The cool air, coupled with the fact she was a bit overtired (having stayed up way too late working on Sue's fairy house), caused her to moan at the thought of getting up, getting ready for the day, and opening the shop. As much as Libby loved the house that had been home to her grandparents, then her grandmother and her quilt shop, there were many times that Libby wished she'd kept her apartment instead of moving into the attic room. It wasn't always the most relaxing circumstance for her—that she slept, ate, lived, *and* worked all in the same building. There were times when Libby felt kind of trapped in the house. She'd quickly realized that she needed get out and go somewhere every day, even if it was just a little walk around the neighborhood. Libby made sure she left the quilt shop and house behind for a little while. The truth was that when she was alive and running the quilt shop, Libby's grandmother had always emphasized the necessity of getting out every day. Libby hadn't really understood why her grandma seemed to nearly harp on the matter to Libby—not until she'd taken ownership of the shop. But once she'd moved into the attic and begun running the shop herself, full awareness washed over her pretty darn fast.

Libby stretched as she lay in bed—smiled with approval as she looked over at the fairy house she'd been working on for Sue. It was coming along just perfectly. From where she sat in bed, she could see into the house—smiled when the sunlight suddenly glinted on the mica flakes glitter she'd added to the pinecone shingles that embellished the herb garden roof of the house. It gave the fairy house the look of being enchanted, and Libby was glad she'd stayed up so late working on the project.

All at once then, a vision of the handsome contractor who would be arriving to meet with her at three p.m. popped into Libby's mind. Suddenly, Libby didn't mind the morning cold or hopping out of bed and having to jump into the shower. After all, Sawyer Delaney was definitely something to look forward to. And in an instant, Libby's day didn't look so chilly and filled with the monotony of routine—whether or not she managed to get out of the house for a while.

♥

"Well, he wasn't wearing a wedding ring," Sue pointed out as she straightened the bolts of fabric on the nursery-themed shelf.

Libby shrugged. "That doesn't mean he's not married."

Shortly after Libby had come downstairs to open the shop that morning, the horrifying realization hit her that perhaps Sawyer Delaney was a married man! She couldn't fathom why she hadn't thought of it before, but once she had thought of it, she felt almost despairing—that was until Sue had arrived, asking her what was the matter, because Libby apparently appeared entirely downtrodden.

Of course, Sue instantly began to reassure Libby that Sawyer Delaney was single and available—to which Libby stated that she shouldn't even care, because it wasn't like the man of her dreams had just walked into her shop by accident, to recognize Libby as the one and only woman he would ever want again.

"Oh, Libby," Sue sighed, "quit being so negative! The man wasn't wearing a wedding ring, he's hot, and besides...I totally believe in love at first sight and that the man of your dreams really *can* just walk into your life." Sue paused and smiled. "In fact, I still think it could happen to me too."

Libby giggled. "Oh, the whole firefighter fantasy thing you have?"

"Yep," Sue assured her friend. "I'll find him one day...or he'll find me. I'm meant to marry a firefighter, and I've known it since I was a little girl." She winked at Libby, adding, "That's why I'm not going to give you any competition where Mr. Hot Buns Contractor is concerned."

"Just because he's not a firefighter?" Libby laughed.

"Yep. There's a handsome firefighter out there for me somewhere. So even though I will admit that your contractor is undeniably lust-provoking, I'm not interested. I'm happy waiting for my firefighter."

"Lust-provoking, Sue?" Libby asked, shaking her head with amusement.

Sue laughed. "Let's just say you're lucky he's not a firefighter, or I'd be melting all over him like fresh butter in a hot skillet."

Again Libby laughed. "Where do you come up with this stuff?" she asked. "And besides, I know you too well. You're all talk...not fresh butter."

Sue 4nodded. "I know, but it's fun to pretend I'm a seductress."

"Oh, I'm sure when the right firefighter comes along, you will be," Libby assured her friend.

"Maybe," Sue admitted. "But what about you? Maybe he is the right flannel-shirt-clad contractor. So what're you going to do about it?"

Libby sighed. "Try not to drool when I'm talking to him this afternoon," she answered. Then with a grin and a shrug, she added, "And maybe find out for *sure* that he's not married."

"And then what?" Sue prodded with excitement.

But Libby shook her head. "I don't know...get to know him better. That won't be hard at *all*, considering the fact he'll be working every second he's here."

"Enough with the sarcasm," Sue said. "And anyway, he has to stop to eat and use the restroom, right?"

"Eat, maybe," Libby said. "But men have bladders the size of Lake Michigan, so I doubt that he'll take the time to use our restroom." She frowned and giggled. "And besides, what am I supposed to do? Hold a conversation with him while he's on the other side of the closed bathroom door, taking care of his...necessities?"

"Of course not, you idiot," Sue began. "You flirt with him on his way to and from the bathroom."

"Oh, you mean buzz around him like one of those annoying flies that seem to attach themselves to you when you're walking down by the river. Yeah, that'll lure him in all right. 'Be a Pest' has always been my motto when it comes to getting guys," Libby said. When Sue sighed and shook her head with disapproving discouragement, Libby offered, "Don't worry. If he's single, I'll…I'll find a way to talk to him and get his attention."

"Wow!" Sue teased. "This Sawyer Delaney guy really did untangle your tinsel, hmmm?"

Libby puffed a breathy laugh. "Yes, Sue…he untangled my tinsel. He's holding my attention captive. He's got me dangling by a string. He's—"

"Yeah, yeah, yeah. I get it…too many metaphors," Sue said. Frowning, she asked, "Or are they idioms?"

"Maybe idioms?" Libby asked. "I'm really not sure. English lit was way too long ago."

"Either way, he's hot, he's not married, and neither are you," Sue stated. "So when he comes in today, start the groundwork for reeling him into your nest."

"Um, Sue…you *have* seen him, right?" Libby teased. "He's…like, gorgeous."

Sue shrugged. "So? Gorgeous guys are real people too, Libby Meadows. For crying out loud, don't write him off just because he's good-looking. Go for it!"

"Says the woman who won't look twice at a guy if he's not a firefighter," Libby reminded her friend. "You're all confident that I should cozy up to Sawyer because *you* aren't the one having to get up the guts to do it."

"That's exactly right," Sue agreed. "I'm the cheerleader here...not the subject who needs cheering."

"True," Libby admitted. "Okay. Okay. When Mr. Hot Buns Contractor comes in to show me his designs, I'll find out if he's married...or has a girlfriend. Then if he's free of any romantic emotional attachments, maybe I'll...maybe I'll try to find little moments to talk to him and stuff."

"Oh, and bring him turkey turds," Sue suggested. "If the hot chocolate you make didn't hook him, a fresh batch of turkey turds will."

"First things first," Libby reminded. "First I find out if he's single. Then if he is, I'll woo him with my turkey turds."

"Awesome!" Sue exclaimed. "I guarantee your turkey turds won't fail you. Julia Child would be proud."

Libby laughed, rolled her eyes, and headed toward the juvenile fabric wall. She smiled as she removed a bolt of jungle-print fabric and straightened it a bit. Maybe Sue was right. After all, even gorgeous men were real people. They had to have friends, family, drama, joy—romance even. Why shouldn't she get to know Sawyer Delaney and see where things went? *If* he wasn't attached, of course. Yet somehow Libby sensed that he wasn't. Somehow Libby knew that once Sawyer arrived for their conference about the designs for the renovation, she would indeed discover that he wasn't married.

Her heart leapt with the ridiculous hope a woman feels when she discovers a man that might be the one of her dreams. Shaking her head, she tried to dispel her silly schoolgirl thoughts about Sawyer maybe finding an interest in her. There was work to do—and a lot of it.

"I'm heading back to finish Mrs. Blair's quilt," Libby said to Sue as she placed the jungle-print fabric back on its shelf.

"Okay," Sue answered. "I'm sure she'll be in soon wanting it to be finished. Yesterday she was all about finding the perfect fat quarters…but you know how Mrs. Blair is."

"Yes, I do. She's got a mind that drifts along sailing every which way the wind blows," Libby confirmed.

"Hmmm…comparing Mrs. Blair's mind to a sailing ship. Is *that* a metaphor?" Sue asked.

"I have no idea," Libby admitted as she headed back to the quilting room to finish Mrs. Blair's quilt.

♥

Libby glanced up at the clock across the room—just as she'd been doing every few minutes since she'd finished lunch. It seemed three p.m. would never arrive. But now it was 2:58, and her heart leapt in her chest as she heard the shop's front door bell tinkle.

Her breath caught in her throat as she turned to see Sawyer Delaney step into the shop. Wow! He was so attractive! She noted he wore a red flannel shirt and wondered how soft and warm it would feel to touch.

Sawyer smiled at her and greeted, "Hi. You ready to choose some designs?"

"As ready as I'll ever be," she answered. Sue looked up from the table where she was cutting fabric for a customer.

"I've got this," she told Libby. "No worries."

Libby knew there were two more customers in the shop, but as she glanced at each of them in turn, she was fairly certain it would be a while before they needed fabric cut. Sue should be fine in the store on her own for a while.

"Let's go to the kitchen," Libby said to Sawyer. "There's hot cider today…or pumpkin bread, if you like."

"Sounds great," he said, nodding at her to indicate he would follow her.

As she led him to the kitchen, Libby hoped her hair looked okay from the back.

"We can just sit at the table and discuss things," she said. "Would you like pumpkin bread or cider or both?"

"Both," Sawyer answered, smiling. "Cute table and chairs," he said, taking a seat at the table tucked away in the breakfast nook.

"Thanks," Libby said. "They were my grandparents'. I ate more cinnamon rolls and drank more glasses of milk right there where you're sitting than I care to count."

She placed a small glass plate piled with three small slices of pumpkin bread on the table in front of Sawyer. She then returned and ladled some mulled cider from the pan steaming on the stove and into a large mug.

Returning to the table, she set the mug near Sawyer's plate of pumpkin bread and took a seat in the chair across from him.

"You're not having some?" he asked as he picked up a piece of pumpkin bread and took a bite.

"Are you kidding?" Libby asked with a giggle. "Do I really look like I need one more ounce of pumpkin bread settling on these hips?"

Immediately she inwardly scolded herself for making reference to her body. He'd think she was trying to provoke a compliment from him or something.

"Doesn't look to me like you've had any pumpkin bread settling on them...not at all," he said, winking at her.

Libby blushed and rather apologetically offered, "Thanks...but I wasn't fishing for a compliment. I just meant...I meant..."

"I know," Sawyer said. "I have three teenage sisters."

He winked at her again when she smiled at him with appreciation.

"So? What have you got for me?" she asked.

Dusting his hands on the front of his flannel shirt (for Libby had neglected to offer him a napkin), he said, "I've got digital renderings for you to look at. I did three for you. I'm sure you'll like one of the three. At least, I hope you will."

"I'm certain I will," Libby assured him.

Reaching down into a black bag he'd brought in with him, Sawyer retrieved a slim laptop. He set it on the table, opened it, and pulled up a program Libby had never seen before. Almost instantly, a virtual design of her renovated sewing instruction room appeared.

"Wow!" Libby gasped as Sawyer turned the computer toward her so she could better view the screen.

"Yeah…this is my favorite," he explained. "Let's start with the floor. I do want to point out that you've got the original wood floor in that room, and it would be sad to just tile or carpet over it. There has been water damage or something to one part of it—which is probably why they painted the floor in the first place. We'll need to strip the old paint off the floor, replace the bad boards, and stain the floor again. But the finished product will be better than this digital rendering. It'll look like it did when the house was new—which, as you know, was in 1891…over a hundred years ago."

"And you think you can restore the floor so that it looks like this one?" Libby asked, pointing to the floor on the virtual room on the computer. "It's gorgeous!"

"Yep, it is…well, it was. But it can be again," Sawyer answered. "Of course, a few of the boards will be new. But only you and me will know that, right?" he asked, smiling at her.

"Right," she agreed, returning his smile.

"You see here that the fireplace stays pretty much the same," he continued. "As I said, the masonry was excellent, and I'm pretty sure it's not damaged anywhere. But we'll have it checked out all the same." He pointed to the sewing stations on the rendering and said, "I've got six sewing stations here, the way you specified, and thought that maybe you'd like a little counter and small sink over here, with some electrical outlets so that you don't have to keep the hot chocolate or whatever sequestered in the kitchen. That way, the…well, I guess you would call them sewing students can serve themselves if you want them to be able to."

He paused, grinned at her, and added, "You seem to be pretty into lulling your customers into a sense of comfort and relaxation…so I figured you might want your students to feel similarly."

"Uh oh. You're onto me," she teased.

"Oh, I'm onto you…believe me," he rather mumbled as he hit something on the keyboard, causing a different rendering to appear.

Of course, Libby could hardly concentrate on the next rendering, because what had he meant by saying he was onto her in the manner in which he had said it? Did he mean he was so good at his job that he could read his clients like a book? Or did he mean something else? Had he sensed she was attracted to him? She hoped not! But then again, she couldn't imagine there was ever a woman whose path he crossed who wasn't attracted to him.

Sawyer jolted her back to the conversation she should be having with him when he said, "As far as a color scheme, I just went with colors that you've already incorporated into your shop. I'm sure you want this instruction area to simply flow with everything else. Right?"

"Right," Libby affirmed. "Did three teenage sisters teach you that?"

He smiled. "Yep…and an interior designer for a mom."

"Oh, wow! And I'm sure your resources don't stop there," Libby said.

"Nope," Sawyer said. Lowering his voice to a conspiratorial tone, he added, "I've got resources that don't even know they're resources."

"Is that so?" Libby asked, smiling at his charming way of drawing her in so thoroughly. "Like, what do you mean? A wife, girlfriend, grandmother?" she tried to probe nonchalantly.

Sawyer shook his head. "Nope. No wife, at the moment no girlfriend, and my grandmothers both really only care about crocheting and watching reality TV. Nope, I mean secret resources…like the kind you're about to become."

"Me?" Libby giggled.

"Yep," he assured her. "I'm taking this big renovation job just a few blocks down from here, and the lady wants it restored and fully staged in a 1930s-style décor. I figure you're gonna be the one who consults with me about what kind of quilts people would've had on their kids' beds back in 1932, right?"

He smiled at her—flashed a dazzling smile that she figured must give him some kind of mind control—for without pause, she answered, "Right."

"That's what I thought," he said, still smiling. "See? I've got my secret resources cached away everywhere."

Libby's smile broadened. She liked the idea of being one of Sawyer Delaney's secret resources. Furthermore, she'd been assured that he definitely did not have a wife—or even a girlfriend.

She studied him a moment as he pulled up another virtual remodel design. Maybe crazy, unbelievable stuff really did happen in life. Maybe Sue O'Shannon was meant to find her firefighter. And maybe Sawyer Delaney…well, maybe the man of her dreams really had simply walked into Libby's quilt shop one bright autumn day.

♥

Libby finished placing the three-footed teacup in just the right spot in the fairy house. Carefully she folded the tiny terrycloth towel and draped it over the little bench she'd fashioned out of twigs and twine.

She sighed, satisfied that any fairy would enjoy a nice long soak in the teacup and wrapping up in the small terrycloth towel that waited afterward. Sue was going to love the fairy house! Of course, there was still a lot to be done—the entire kitchen, the lounging area, and Libby wanted to add a few more tiny LED lights to the ceiling. But it was coming right along, and she was pleased with it.

Of course, nothing could please her more than the half an hour meeting with Sawyer Delaney that had turned into an hour and a half! For the first time since taking over the shop, Libby was glad the quilt shop had been a little slow with customers that afternoon. Otherwise, Sue would've really had her hands full while Libby had been meeting with Sawyer.

Having already brushed her teeth, washed her face, and pulled on her pajamas, Libby left Sue's fairy house and crawled into bed. She turned off the lamp that was on her nightstand, lay down, and turned onto her right side so that she could gaze at the stars through the attic window. She pulled the covers up to her neck, wishing she trusted the old fireplace in the room enough to build a fire in it to warm her. Yet she'd be warm enough.

The moon was full and lent a soft yellow glow to the cozy attic room. Libby wondered what kind of a house or apartment Sawyer lived in. Was he gazing out some window looking at the same moon and thinking that the large golden moon of autumn was the most beautiful of the year?

Rolling her eyes at such a ridiculous notion as any man noticing what any season's moon looked like, Libby sighed and thought about the fact that the renovation began at eight a.m. the next morning. She couldn't wait!

Sawyer's designs had all been marvelous, and Libby had easily decided on the one he'd preferred and recommended—because she had preferred it too. When it was all said and done, the renovated room would be inviting, cozy, and wonderfully functional—a brilliant and valuable addition to the quilt shop.

Libby gazed out the attic window for a few more moments, until her eyelids grew heavy and begged for sleep.

"It will be so pretty in there when he's finished," she mumbled as she relaxed and began to drift. She grinned a little. "And he doesn't even have a girlfriend."

CHAPTER FOUR

The next morning, Sawyer and his renovation crew arrived at eight a.m. sharp. Libby didn't know whether to be impressed or insulted when, instead of lingering in talking to her for a few minutes, Sawyer got right to work on prepping for the renovation. Obviously he was an ethical and diligent worker. But also obvious was the fact that he was there only to work—not to socialize with Libby.

Admittedly Libby was disappointed with not being able to even say more than, "Good morning," to Sawyer. Yet he had been hired to work, not to entertain. Therefore, Libby tried to stay busy for the first part of the day—tried not to wish Sawyer would stick his head out of the renovation area to at least say hello again.

Just before lunch, Libby knew she'd failed miserably in hiding her discontent, however, because Sue said, "He's here to do a job, Libby. He can't spend the *whole* time sitting in the kitchen eating pumpkin bread with you, you know. What would that do to his reputation as a contractor, hmmm?"

Libby shook her head. "Am I that pitifully obvious?" she asked Sue.

"Only to me," Sue assured her. "I'm thinking your neck must be sore from craning around to look in the direction of the remodel."

Libby sighed with self-disgust. "You're right. I'm a dork." She shook her head again, irritated with herself for being so focused on the fact that the man of her dreams was working in the other room. She had a business to run, for crying out loud.

"You're not a dork," Sue argued. "You're a huntress...and you're keeping your eye on your prey."

"What?" Libby exclaimed. She giggled. "Okay, I think I'd rather be a dork than a huntress."

"No, you wouldn't," Sue assured her. "Look, Libby," she began, surprising Libby with her uncharacteristically serious expression. "If you don't snatch up this guy, some other chick will. What? You just want to let him waltz into your life, do a renovation for your business, and waltz out and into the arms of some other woman?"

"You're reminding me that I should at least try to get to know him, see if I like him and if...if he might like me back. I know. And you're right," Libby admitted. "But it's hard, you know. Especially when he's here to work."

"I know," Sue admitted. "But try hanging your hopes on the fact that the next guy who walks through the door will be a fireman."

And then—as if the Fates themselves had shown up to intervene in their sarcastic, eleventh-hour way—Sawyer stepped into the room. "Hey, Libby. We're getting ready to pull up those damaged floorboards," he said. "If we're going to find something cool hidden away, my experience tells me that this is your chance. Wanna come watch…just in case?"

Libby shot a playful glare at Sue before answering, "Sure."

"And there it is…opportunity knocking," Sue whispered as Libby put down the rotary cutters she'd been using to cut fat quarters.

As she followed Sawyer into the room being renovated, he warned, "Now about sixty percent of the time there's something under these old floors…but mostly just ancient newspaper and stuff people used to stuff in to help insulate. But sometimes there are old medicine bottles and things. So don't get your hopes up. I wanted to bring you in, just in case."

Libby smiled at him. After all, it was a very thoughtful gesture.

"Thanks," she said. "And I won't get my hopes up…even though they kind of already are."

Sawyer chuckled a bit. "I know what you mean."

He nodded to a guy who was holding a crowbar, and Libby watched with an excited anticipation she could not squelch.

As one workman pried up a damaged floorboard, another pulled on it and removed it.

"Well…that's kind of scary," Libby said, "that they come up so easily."

"They're not nailed into a subflooring like we do nowadays. These were just laid on top of intermediate boards and nailed to those," Sawyer explained.

Libby couldn't keep from peering down into the space beneath the floor as the men removed more of the damaged wood.

"Looks like newspaper," Sawyer explained.

Libby felt exhilaration rising in her and turned to him, asking, "Can I pull one of the newspapers out?"

Sawyer smiled, obviously pleased by her enthusiasm. "Of course."

"How old do you think these are?" she asked, kneeling down and pulling out one of the ancient, crumpled papers. Carefully spreading the paper open, Libby squealed with delight as a rendering of a woman dressed in the recognizable fashion of a Gibson Girl looked back at her. "*Harper's Bazaar*...November 20, 1897! How fun!"

"And look," Sawyer said, pointing to a space between another board his guys had just removed. "Looks like you've got some editions that aren't crumpled up...like they just laid them in there."

Squealing again, Libby reached into the revealed space beneath the old floorboards and retrieved an edition of *Harper's Bazaar* magazine, entirely intact. The ancient paper was yellowed but in magnificent shape otherwise.

"Oh, I love this!" Libby exclaimed. Delving in to retrieve more magazines, she paused, gasping when, beneath a short stack of antique *Harper's Bazaar* magazines, she found a book—and the title of the book immediately caught her attention and interest.

"No way!" she breathed. "No way!"

Looking over her shoulder, Sawyer said, "*Dracula?*"

"Yes! Can you even believe this?" Libby giggled. "Ha ha! How scandalous!"

"Scandalous?" Sawyer asked as Libby carefully removed the book.

"Yes, scandalous," Libby affirmed. "The Victorians were all about poetry and drama and gothic stories. And when *Dracula* was first published, it didn't do that well...mostly because it was considered scandalous!"

"Why? Because of all the neck biting or what?" Sawyer asked.

"Yes...well, in part," Libby explained. "At that time, the book was considered to be kind of a...you know, encouraging to women to be...you know...wanton."

"Sexually aggressive," Sawyer summarized with a nod of understanding.

"Yeah," Libby affirmed, blushing.

Opening the book, she looked at the copyright page. "Holy smokes!" she exclaimed. "It's dated May 27, 1897!"

"Wow, that is old," Sawyer agreed.

"No, I mean...I did a paper on this book in college. I think this is a first edition," Libby explained.

"Sweet," Sawyer chuckled. "So we did find you some buried treasure after all."

"Indeed, you did," Libby mumbled as she studied the book. "And look at this inscription. *To my dearest, Lucille. Let this be our sisters' secret. Lovingly and Always, Your Sister Hattie. July 12, 1897.* Holy smokes!" Libby breathed in awe.

"Looks like that's probably all that's down there," Sawyer commented as the men removed the last board to be replaced.

"All? All?" Libby exclaimed. "It's the best! And way better than old tonic bottles or whatever you usually find. I just can't believe it's so well preserved, especially since you said the boards show water damage."

Sawyer shook his head and shrugged his broad shoulders. "I guess the water just warped the boards and messed up the finish...but didn't seep through to the magazines and books."

Giggling with the delight produced by pure adrenalin, Libby reached over, throwing her arms around Sawyer's neck and hugging him. "Thank you so much! Thank you!" she giggled. "Holy smokes, what a find! Thank you, Sawyer."

"Well, I'm not the one who put them there," he said, returning her embrace. "But you're welcome all the same."

Hopping to her feet, Libby looked to the two men who had removed the damaged boards. "Thanks so much, you guys. Wow, I'm so...like...overwhelmed! Thank you!" Then wagging an index finger at the two men, she added, "There are fresh pumpkin cookies in the kitchen today, you guys. Be sure you load up sometime today, okay? It's the only way I know to show my thanks to you guys." She looked back to Sawyer, adding, "All of you guys. Thanks, Sawyer."

Sawyer smiled as Libby gathered up the old *Harper's Bazaar* magazines. She was legitimately wowed about what she'd found beneath the old floorboards—and he was glad. He'd been very fearful that all they'd find was an old mouse's nest or something, and he'd wanted there to be something cool under the floor—something cool for Libby to find. In fact, he'd wanted her to be able to find something sort of treasure-ish in the old house she owned, more than anyone else he'd ever renovated an old house for.

"A first edition of Bram Stoker's *Dracula*! Can you imagine?" Libby chirped, still smiling. "Wait until I tell Sue! And my dad will freak out. I love this!"

"I'm glad someone left something for you to find in here, Libby," Sawyer said.

"Me too," she said, hugging him once more. "Well, I better let you guys get back to work." Glancing up to Mike and Dwight, she added, "And don't forget the pumpkin cookies in the kitchen, okay?"

"Yes, ma'am," Mike said with a nod.

"We'll be sure to indulge," Dwight added.

"Thanks again for calling me in here, Sawyer," Libby said as she turned to leave. "You made my day!"

"Good," Sawyer said as he watched her go.

"Falling for the boss's daughter already, Sawyer?" Mike teased.

"Dude, boss's daughter nothing! She *is* the boss, remember?" Dwight corrected.

"Oh, that's right," Mike said, nodding. "Setting your sights pretty high…going for the boss lady. I mean, all that hugging and groping and stuff. Man, you're slick."

"She hugged *me*, remember?" Sawyer pointed out. "And there was no groping involved."

"Bummer, man," Dwight said.

"No kidding," Sawyer joked. "Let's get the rest of the floor stripped and sanded so we can get this done."

But even as Sawyer helped get the old wood floor ready for a facelift, he couldn't keep from thinking about Libby. The fact was he thought about her all the time—since the moment he'd met her. He was finding that it was pretty difficult to stay focused on work when he knew she was just a couple of rooms away.

There weren't too many people who intimidated Sawyer Delaney, but for some reason, Libby Meadows did. She was young, capable, and owned her own business—but that wasn't it. She was really pretty and had a great figure—but that wasn't it. What *was* it was that in his gut, Sawyer worried that if he made a play for her, she'd reject him. Oh sure, he'd faced rejection from girls or women his entire life; every guy did, from the moment he had his first crush. But that was part of the whole dating game, of wading through the misery until finding the one person that fit best. Still, for some reason, the idea of asking Libby Meadows out stalled his confidence. If he got to know Libby better, started really, really liking her, and then she rejected him, Sawyer felt like he might not recover from it.

And yet she seemed to like him well enough. She didn't start gagging or anything when she looked at him. She'd even hugged him when she'd found the book under the old floor. And although Sawyer totally understood that girls hugging guys didn't mean they wanted to be asked out by them, he'd noted it wasn't a "I'm just hugging you to be nice" hug—but more of a "I'm really grateful, and I like hugging you" hug—actually hugs, plural. After all, his sisters had spent three hours one evening explaining to him the different kinds of hugs girls offered, and he was fairly certain that Libby's hugs were inviting ones and not the kind a woman gives to an ugly dog she feels sorry for.

He wondered then if maybe he should wait until the reno job was over before pursuing Libby—*if* he could work up the nerve at all. Maybe it was tacky to ask her out while he was working for her, or maybe she had a personal rule about not dating the help—though he didn't think she was the sort to be stuck up.

Exhaling a heavy sigh, Sawyer shook his head. It was a quandary he'd have to think about later. For now, there was work to be done—work for Libby, the cute quilt shop owner.

As Libby returned to the front of the store still excited about the book and magazines Sawyer and his guys had unearthed, Sue stopped her short, right in front of the kitchen.

"FYI, Libby," Sue whispered, "Eric Dawson just walked in."

Libby grimaced and moaned, "Oh no. Not now."

"Oh…would there ever be a better time?" Sue whispered with thick sarcasm. "I warned you this would happen."

"I know, I know," Libby mumbled.

Sue sighed. "Well, you might as well face the music, Libs. Just get it over with."

"Okay," Libby sighed. "But look what Sawyer found under the floor in there first."

Handing Sue one of the *Harper's Bazaar* magazines, she smiled when Sue's eyes lit up like Christmas lights.

"Wow! No way!" Sue exclaimed.

"I know, right?" Libby said, smiling again. "And there's a book that I think might be a first edition."

As she handed the book to Sue as well, Sue giggled, "Oooo, *Dracula*! How scandalous!"

"I know, I can't believe it! I can't wait to look through everything," Libby admitted. Then, glancing past Sue to where Eric Dawson stood waiting for her, Libby sighed, handed the entire stack of magazines to Sue, and said, "Will you put these somewhere safe until I have some free time to really enjoy them, please?"

"You bet," Sue agreed. "Oh, and Mrs. Blair called. She's coming in for her quilt in a while, okay?"

"Yeah. I finished it yesterday," Libby mumbled.

Sue glanced back to Eric Dawson and then back to Libby. "Just tell him you're busy. I mean, you've got a remodel going and quilting to do; there's that new inventory in the back."

Libby nodded. "I will. But he's always so persistent. It gives me a stomachache."

Sue watched as Libby headed toward the front of the store where Eric Dawson stood waiting for her. She shook her head with sympathy. Poor Libby! Still, Sue had warned her BFF before she'd agreed to go on a date with Eric: mercy dates only led to big fat messes.

Sue heard the sound of some electric tool start up in the room being renovated at the back of the house, and suddenly she felt the warm smile spurred by a devious idea spreading across her face. Libby had gotten herself into a big pickle where Eric Dawson was concerned. But thankfully, she had Sue O'Shannon for a best friend.

As Sue made her way back to the renovation area, she couldn't help but giggle, pleased over her own mischief.

"Hey," she said as she stepped into the renovation area. One of the guys was on his hands and knees using an electric sander on the floor, looked up, and turned off the sander.

"Yeah?" another guy asked.

Sawyer turned around then. "Something wrong?" he asked.

"Kind of," Sue answered. Smiling directly at Sawyer then, she asked, "Are you up to and willing to save a damsel in distress, Mr. Delaney?"

"Hey, Libby!" Eric greeted with an enthusiasm that gave Libby the willies. "I haven't seen you in forever...so I thought I'd stop in and say hi."

"Well, that's sweet of you, Eric," Libby greeted. "Unfortunately, it's kind of a busy day," Libby fibbed.

"It is?" Eric asked, glancing around the shop where not one single customer was lingering at the moment.

"Well, in the back," Libby stammered. "I'm working with the quilting machine, and we're...we're having a renovation done, and the contractor and his guys are here. So I guess it just feels a lot more crazy than it is."

"Well, can you take a lunch break? Or do you have to babysit the contractor?" Eric asked in the sarcastic, accusing tone Libby hated in him.

"I wasn't planning on taking a lunch today," Libby fibbed again. "I'm just swamped, Eric."

Eric paused, his eyes narrowing with suspicion. "You know, every time I come in, it seems you never have time for me," he accused.

The feeling of nausea in Libby's stomach increased. Why, oh why, had she ever agreed to go out with him? It seemed harmless enough at the time. Eric Dawson had been asking her out for over a year, and excuses as to why she couldn't go with him were wearing thin. So one day Libby accepted his offer, thinking that one date would either satisfy him or deter him. But all it had done was give him false hope, and he'd been hounding Libby ever since.

It wasn't that Eric wasn't a nice guy—he was. He was even a pretty good-looking man. But it was just— well, she just wasn't attracted to him at all. Furthermore, there was something about Eric that sent Libby's senses screaming at her to flee. So, in the end, she'd made the mistake of agreeing to go out with him once, assuming he would lose interest in her and move on. But going out with him only proved the old adage true, about what happens when the word "assume" is broken down; assuming Eric would lose interest after one mercy date made a fool out of Eric as well as Libby. The date had encouraged Eric rather than discouraged him, and now he lingered on the brink of stalking Libby. At least it was the way he made Libby feel.

"I'm sorry, Eric. It's just that…well, you know I run this place now, and it takes all my time," she explained. "I really am swamped."

Literal goose bumps of relief erupted over Libby's arms and legs then as she heard Sawyer's voice from behind her.

"Libby?" he began. "I need you back in the reno area for a while. We ran into a problem, and there are some design changes we need to make."

Libby tried not to enjoy the scowl that puckered Eric's brow as he looked past her, glaring at Sawyer—but she did enjoy it.

Turning to face Sawyer, momentarily stunned into silence by how hot he looked standing there in his work boots, worn jeans, flannel shirt, and tool belt, she said, "Okay...I'll be right there."

She was even more thrilled when Sawyer stood where he was, folded his muscular arms across his broad chest, stared down Eric, and said, "I'll wait right here for you."

Turning back to Eric, knowing there was no way he could miss the expression of delight seeing Sawyer had plastered on her face, she said, "You see, Eric? My life is the business now. I really don't have time for...for anything else...even lunch."

Eric looked to Libby and back to Sawyer. "This guy is your contractor? What? Did you have contractors submit their bids in the nude or something?"

Anxiety leapt to Libby's chest as she realized that Eric was furious.

"No, she didn't," Sawyer answered for her. "But if she had...I still would've had the best bid that way too." Sawyer stepped forward then, glaring at Eric. "Now why don't you haul your white-collar ass out that door and leave the lady alone. She's not interested, man."

"How do you know she's not interested?" Eric growled, straightening his posture. "If she's not interested, she can tell me herself."

He looked to Libby then, and a strange sort of terror began to engulf her. Eric's eyes were nearly red with fury.

"If you don't want to go out with me again, just tell me, Libby," Eric growled. "I have other fish I can fry."

Libby glanced back to see that Sawyer had moved closer to her and now stood directly behind her. He gave her a quick nod of encouragement, as if to silently say, *Send him packing. I've got your back.*

Turning her attention back to Eric, Libby forced out, "I-I really...I really don't want to go out with you again, Eric. I'm so sorry, but I—"

"That's all you had to say, Libby," Eric interrupted. "You keep slumming with your muscle-bound contractor there. I'm finished with you."

Whirling around, Eric yanked open the quilt shop door and stormed away.

Libby turned to face Sawyer once more to see Sue standing next to him, smiling with triumph.

"You guys just saved my bacon," Libby said as understanding washed over her.

"You bet we did," Sue confirmed.

Libby smiled at Sawyer. "So I take it the remodel designs are fine?"

"Of course," Sawyer answered. He nodded toward Sue and added, "Your friend here has your six, that's all."

Sue frowned and looked to Sawyer. "I have her six?"

Libby laughed. "Think of a clock, Sue. I'm the twelve, and you're the six?" When Sue still looked perplexed, Libby explained, "You have my back. You look out for me?"

"Oh yeah!" Sue exclaimed. "That's me! Always watching your six."

"I think the dude that just left was the one always watching Libby's six," he teased, winking at Libby.

Libby's smile faded. "You don't think Eric will, like, try to murder me or something, huh?"

But Sue rolled her eyes and sighed, "No, Libby. You watch too many cop shows."

"He'll leave you alone now," Sawyer offered. "But it sounds like you got burned the way we all do at some point. Mercy dates only lead to drama."

"Obviously," Libby admitted. She tipped her head to one side and studied the hot contractor with the blue eyes for a moment. "So...are you saying you've fallen victim to the mercy date curse?"

"Yep," he answered. "Senior year...a girl named Heather." He shook his head. "It was a nightmare. It was awful and got a lot worse than this...so don't feel bad."

Libby nodded with renewed humility. She still felt bad for Eric, but she knew it was best to just be brutally honest with him and send him on his way.

"Thanks, you guys," she said, looking from Sawyer to Sue and back. "You guys have both certainly earned a piece of the pumpkin roll I hid in the fridge in the kitchen today."

"You brought one of your pumpkin rolls and didn't tell me?" Sue exclaimed, slamming her fists onto her hips in scolding Libby.

Libby shrugged. "Well, yeah. And I wanted it to last until lunch so we could share it with...you know...whoever. Last year when I brought it, the two of us had scarfed it down before ten a.m."

"True," Sue admitted, frowning. "Okay, I forgive you."

Sawyer glanced up at the clock on the wall. "Well, it's time for the guys to break for lunch anyway." He frowned and asked, "Pumpkin roll, you say?"

Libby nodded.

He smiled. "Then I'm in. Give me a minute."

"Of course," Libby said.

He turned to head back to the reno area but paused. Glancing over his shoulder to Sue and then Libby, he asked, "Hmmm. Do you ladies think I really would win more bids if I presented them in the nude?"

Libby blushed to the tips of her toes, and then she and Sue both gasped as Mrs. Blair suddenly appeared from between two tall rows of fabric shelves and answered, "Yes."

"Mrs. Blair! I didn't see you come in!" Sue exclaimed.

"That's because I arrived very stealthily just behind Libby's stalker there, while you were talking to Libby," Mrs. Blair explained. "And you, Mr. Contractor...that was very heroic of you to send that Eric packing the way you did."

"Thank you, ma'am," Sawyer said, a bit red-faced himself.

"Furthermore, you've inspired me, young man," Mrs. Blair said.

"I have?" Sawyer asked, obviously perplexed.

"You have," Mrs. Blair assured him.

"But…how did Sawyer inspire you, Mrs. Blair? With his heroics? With his renovation designs?" Libby prodded.

"With both," Mrs. Blair answered.

Sue gasped and giggled and so did Libby as Mrs. Blair reached up to one of the fabric shelves and removed a bolt of fabric.

Holding up fabric printed with artist renderings of shirtless men wearing jeans and tool belts, Mrs. Blair seemed to pause to read the label on the end of the bolt. "This 'Heavy Equipment Pin-Ups' fabric will be perfect for making pillowcases for my teenage granddaughters and their friends for Christmas gifts," she explained. "I figure you'd probably look like one of these muscular, sexy men if you were to strip off that shirt you're wearing right now. So…I'll take six yards, please, Sue."

Libby giggled as Sawyer blushed and Mrs. Blair plopped the bolt of fabric down on the cutting table without cracking a smile.

"I'm off to find contrast fabrics for the pillowcases now," Mrs. Blair announced as she wandered off into the store. "Oh! Make that eight yards, Sue. I'll make an apron for myself out of it too."

Libby and Sue looked to Sawyer, who stood red-faced and wearing an expression of astonishment.

"She's kidding, right?" he whispered.

"Not at all," Libby answered. "She takes all her sewing projects very seriously."

"And I'll have a piece of that hidden pumpkin roll too, Libby," Mrs. Blair called from another fabric aisle.

"Yes, ma'am," Libby laughed.

Sawyer strode over to the cutting table. Lifting the bolt of fabric and pulling a length of it out to investigate, he said, "Wow. Fabric sure has changed since *my* grandma was making pillowcases."

"I suppose it has," Libby admitted, still very amused by Mrs. Blair's antics—and Sawyer's discomfort.

"Let your guys go to lunch, Sawyer," Sue said as she began to unroll fabric off the bolt Mrs. Blair had chosen. "Then meet me and Libby in the kitchen, and we'll get you some of Libby's *hidden* pumpkin roll." She glared playfully at Libby and mumbled, "Brat."

"Okay," Sawyer agreed.

"And...thank you, Sawyer," Libby said to him, "for getting me out of a mess of my own making."

Sawyer smiled and winked at her, sending her heart skipping and butterflies taking flight in her stomach.

"Anytime," he said. "We've all been there." Sawyer took one last look of the shirtless men fabric Sue was measuring out and mumbled, "I guess I should be flattered...I think."

"You should," Libby assured him.

He nodded and walked away.

"What a morning, huh?" Sue asked Libby.

Libby smiled as she watched Sawyer walk away—noting the manner in which his jeans fit so perfectly to his rear end. "Yep. I couldn't have asked for a better one."

CHAPTER FIVE

Every day for the next two weeks, Sawyer Delaney and his crew worked on the renovation at the quilt shop. And every day Libby looked forward to noon when Sawyer would join her in the kitchen to eat.

Sawyer brown-bagged his lunch, and Libby was constantly surprised at what would compose the meal. Most of the time Sawyer's lunch included the leftovers of whatever he'd eaten for dinner the night before (leftover frozen pizza, leftover takeout chicken, leftover takeout Chinese food). Sometimes, however, Sawyer's lunch was a conglomeration of things he'd obviously dug out of his cupboard—for example, a can of green beans coupled with a single-serving cup of peanut butter and a granola bar.

Libby got to where she couldn't wait to see what Sawyer had stuffed in a brown paper bag for lunch on any given day. It was like a perpetual riddle that ended in a complete surprise.

With every lunch hour Libby spent in Sawyer's company, she felt more comfortable with him, learned more about his past and his present, and liked him more and more and more. It seemed everything about Sawyer Delaney had been handpicked to match Libby's idea of the perfect man for her.

Furthermore, Sawyer seemed to enjoy her company as much as she enjoyed his. So for one hour each day—noon to one—Libby savored every moment she spent with him. It seemed they were becoming really good friends, if nothing else.

But every night—after Sue, Sawyer, and his renovation crew were gone and the shop was closed—Libby would find herself up in her cozy attic bedroom, diligently working on all the little details necessary to finish up Sue's fairy house and obsessing over Sawyer.

The fact was she wanted him—like, forever! The more she liked him—the more she fell in love with who he was, the kind of man he was—the more she was certain she might shrivel up and die if she couldn't keep him. And yet he hadn't asked her out or anything—hadn't even implied that he ever would.

Sue's opinion was that Sawyer either lacked the confidence to ask her out for fear of rejection or thought it wasn't kosher to date a woman he was doing a renovation for.

Naturally Libby thought Sue's explanation was absurd—especially when Sue next suggested that Libby be the one to make the first move and ask Sawyer out. Libby had simply laughed out loud and told her friend she was nuts.

"Girls ask guys out all the time these days, Libby," Sue had reminded her. And even though Libby knew it to be true, she was simply too traditional—not to mention fearful of rejection herself—to do it.

Therefore, Sue and Libby began to brainstorm how to inadvertently bump into Sawyer outside of the shop. Sue suggested she and Libby follow him home one night—find out where he lived and then where he shopped for groceries. Sue figured Libby could just happen to bump into Sawyer at the grocery store, and maybe a different meeting place would spur Sawyer on to asking Libby out.

But Libby thought the idea was too sneaky and embarrassing—because there was no way Sawyer would believe Libby just *happened* to be shopping at a store she normally didn't shop at on the very day and moment that Sawyer was shopping.

Nope, Libby was convinced that if Sawyer really did like her as much as Sue claimed he did—or even a fraction of how much Libby liked him—he would eventually ask her out. So she decided to wait—for the time being. And so two weeks had passed, and the last week of the renovation was upon her. One more week and either Sawyer would be out of her life forever, or Libby would have to find a way to hang onto him.

The first day of the last week of the renovation dawned bright and sunny. Quickly, however, clouds began to roll in, and by noon, November had announced its arrival with a steady rain that made Libby want to simply curl up in a chair and read a book.

Oddly, however, it seemed that swarm after swarm of customers visited the shop, and Libby had one of the most successful sales days of the year. In fact, it wasn't until seven p.m. that Libby finally finished cutting the last yardages of fabrics for the last customer.

Libby had let Sue go home at six and finished off the day herself. So when she closed the front door to the shop, it was with a very fatigued and relieved sigh.

"Wow! What a day," she breathed, leaning back against the door once she'd turned the sign to display "Closed" to anyone approaching the shop.

"You can say that again," Sawyer said, unexpectedly appearing from the direction of the renovation.

Libby smiled at the sight of his handsome face, broad shoulders, and everything else that was gorgeous about him.

"I didn't realize you were still here," she greeted.

He grinned. "I know you didn't. You were too busy slicing fabric over there," he said, nodding toward the cutting table. "There were a few details I needed to look over before we start painting tomorrow." He clapped his hands, rubbing them together with excitement. "We're almost there! Are you stoked?"

Libby giggled. "I am," she said—even though she was actually depressed that the reno would soon be done, meaning that Sawyer would be gone.

Sawyer inhaled a deep breath. "Hey, I'm hungry. Did you already eat dinner?" he asked.

"Nope," Libby answered as a hopefulness she tried not to feel began to swell inside her.

"Wanna go grab something with me?" Sawyer asked. "I don't have anything at home that's easy, and if I go to bed hungry, I'll be a bear in the morning."

"I'm starving too," Libby said—even though she'd grabbed three pieces of pumpkin bread before cutting the last customer's fabric.

"Well, grab your jacket, and let's go," Sawyer said. "Does pizza sound okay?"

"Sounds perfect," Libby answered as her excitement mounted. Sure, it wasn't necessarily an official date, per say—but he'd asked her to do something with him, and she was euphoric!

♥

As Libby sat across the table in the booth she was sharing with Sawyer, she couldn't banish the perpetual smile on her face. Sawyer was telling her about a new renovation, another old Victorian house located in the same neighborhood as Libby's quilt shop. This time, however, the renovation involved every part of the house, even some foundation work that needed to be done. From the way he was describing the house and what his designs involved, it was obvious he was very excited about the project. And though Libby was happy for him, her heart began to kind of throb with a dull ache in being reminded that soon Sawyer wouldn't be *her* contractor anymore but someone else's.

And yet her perpetual smile didn't fade—for he was too dreamy to look at, to listen to, and to simply be with. And then—in that very moment—Libby's mind actually surrendered to what her heart had been fighting.

I love him, she thought. *I'm so, so, so in love with him!*

It was the silent admitting to herself that finally slapped the smile from her face—and Sawyer noticed.

His handsome brow puckered with concern. "Are you okay?" he asked.

"Oh yeah," Libby assured him, now forcing her lips to curve up. "I'm just way hungry."

"Me too," Sawyer said, looking over his shoulder in obvious search of their waiter. "But the pizza should be here any second." Looking back to her, he asked, "Do you want me to order some more breadsticks or something?"

"Oh no…not at all," Libby answered. "I'm probably just kind of letting down from the day too, you know? It was kind of crazy."

"Yeah, I noticed that," Sawyer said. "I guess the rainy weather really brings people into the shop, hmmm?"

"Sometimes. Well, this time of year anyway. Not so much in, like, March, you know," Libby began to explain. "By then people are sick of the dreary winter and stuff, and they tend to stay home and vegetate on the couch and watch too much TV. I'm speaking from my own experience, of course."

"I'm not much of a late-winter, early-spring man myself," Sawyer agreed. "It makes my job more difficult for one thing. All the mud…it's a mess."

"I can imagine," Libby said as her smile returned. All she had to do was look at him and she felt better.

Sawyer smiled and leaned over the table toward her. "Wanna hear a joke?" he asked.

Libby giggled. "Of course!"

She could tell by the expression of mischief that sprang to his dreamy blue eyes that he was already amused by the joke and excited to share it with her.

"Okay," he began. "So there's this guy, and he saves all year to go to the Super Bowl."

"Yeah," Libby giggled.

He continued, "He even took an extra job to make enough to buy a ticket to the Super Bowl. It was totally a dream come true...something he'd wanted his entire life."

"Oh, how sweet," Libby sighed.

"Well, the guy kept working the extra job awhile because he needed some cash for his expenses—you know, airfare, hotel, food, stuff like that. Well, finally the day arrived. He hopped on a plane, and pretty soon, there he sat, in the Superdome. He had a good seat too. Seventy-three thousand people there, and he'd managed to snag a seat on the fifty-yard line, about midway up."

"Mmm hmmm," Libby mumbled, in acknowledgement that she was listening to every detail.

"So the game is about to begin," Sawyer continued. "And the guy is stoked when the team he's rooting for wins the coin toss. He figures it's a good start to what will be the greatest experience of his life, you know."

Libby giggled, delighted by Sawyer's excitement.

"The guy's team chooses to receive," Sawyer explains. "Both teams set up for the kickoff. They start running—and just then, as the kicker kicks the ball, our guy hears someone behind him yell, 'Hey, Dave! How'd you get tickets to the Super Bowl?' Our guy turns around but doesn't recognize anybody, right? And when he turns back around, it turns out he'd missed the kickoff *and* a fumble by his team, because the refs are saying that the other team has possession of the ball now. Man, he was ticked! Getting to the Super Bowl was like a dream…then missing the kickoff? It stunk."

"Poor thing," Libby sympathized.

"But he was a positive kind of guy, and after a moment he figured, hey, he's got the whole Super Bowl to enjoy, so what does it matter if he missed the kickoff, right? Pretty soon a vendor came down the aisle selling popcorn. So the guy decided to get a snack, a nice bag of warm Superdome popcorn. But as he starts to take a piece, again someone behind him yells, 'Hey, Dave! Seriously, how did you get here, man?' And it startled him so badly that he jostled the bag of popcorn and spilled all of it—every last popped and buttery kernel. Of course, he was really irritated. He stood up, turned around, and searched the crowd for a familiar face but still couldn't see who had called out."

"How sad," Libby moaned with disappointment.

"I know, huh," Sawyer agreed. "Well, he was really ticked off. But being the optimist he was, he settled back into the game. Pretty soon he sees another vendor coming down the aisle, this time selling peanuts. By now he's pretty hungry, so he waved the vendor over and bought some peanuts. With a heavy sigh of contentment, he opened his bag of peanuts and started eating them. They were freshly roasted, warm, and salty, and the first taste was awesome! But then, again, someone from behind him yelled, 'Hey, Dave!' and in his hurry to turn around to try and see who was calling, he spilled his peanuts all over the bleachers and onto the dirty concrete floor."

"Oh no!" Libby moaned and giggled simultaneously. She figured the joke must really have a great punch line, for Sawyer's facial expression was becoming more and more delighted by the second.

"Well, the dude still had some money left, so when the beverages vendor showed up, the dude blew the rest of his wad on a twenty-ounce pop. It was cold and refreshing, but about the time he'd swallowed the first gulp...you've probably already guessed, the same voice, only seeming closer now, came from somewhere behind him. 'Hey, Dave!' And there went the pop, all over the dude's lap."

Libby shook her head in unison with Sawyer's as Sawyer sighed, "Well, needless to say, he'd had it."

"Needless to say," Libby repeated.

"The dude had worked two jobs, saved all year for his Super Bowl ticket. And now he had nothing to eat, nothing to drink, and judging by the score on the scoreboard, his team was going to lose. So as he sat with the front of his shirt all wet and sticky, he heard it again—someone from somewhere close behind him shout, 'Hey, Dave!' Well, that was it! He'd come so far, sacrificed so much, and some idiot had ruined the whole game for him. So standing up and turning around, furious, he shouted, 'Hey, moron! My name's not Dave!'"

Sawyer sat back in his chair then, smiling and chuckling to himself as if the joke were over. Libby frowned a moment—but only a moment—because then it hit her, the punch line of his favorite joke.

"His name wasn't even *Dave*?" she asked as she began to giggle. "All that? And his name wasn't Dave? He wasn't even the guy the other person was yelling at?"

It hit her full-throttle then, the ridiculousness of the joke, the ingenious ridiculousness of it.

"Ah ha ha!" Libby began to laugh. Realizing how loud she was laughing, she put a hand over her mouth as more laughter overtook her. "My name's not Dave!" she laughed. Then as she was absolutely lost to mirthful amusement, she jogged her feet on the floor underneath her chair as her back began to hurt from the wild glee that was consuming her in that moment.

If there was one thing about Libby Meadows that was truer than any other, it was that she loved to laugh. Furthermore, when a good round of laughter washed over her, it wasn't easy to stop. Pressing her forehead to the tabletop as she continued to laugh, she gently slapped her hand on the table beside her head as reel after reel of pealing laughter consumed her.

She could hear Sawyer laughing as well but couldn't see through the tears of amusement in her eyes whether he was laughing at her or with her.

"My name's not Dave! Ah ha ha ha ha!" Libby gasped.

Sawyer was entirely pulled into waves of laughter as he watched Libby's reaction to his joke—his favorite joke—a joke that very few people ever got, let alone thought was funny. But Libby had gotten it. In fact, she'd more than gotten it—she'd thought it was as funny as Sawyer did. Nobody could fake the kind of laughter she was embroiled in across the table from him. The tears of mirth were streaming from the corners of her eyes, and she couldn't catch a good breath. And when she did catch a breath and her laughter started to subside a bit, she'd simply spurt out, "My name's not Dave!" and find herself overcome with what appeared to be almost painful laughter all over again.

It was obvious that Libby Meadows was not afraid to laugh—not too proud or worried what people would think of her, to laugh at something she truly found funny. And the truth of that was simply another thing that added to her overall attractiveness. A good sense of humor and the absence of excessive pride were rare—things Sawyer admired in anyone, especially a woman.

Sawyer laughed some more as he watched her, entirely pleased and amused by her reaction to his Dave joke.

"It wasn't that funny," he offered in an attempt to calm her, for he was getting worried that she'd pass out from being unable to breathe properly.

"Yes, it was," she choked out, however. "My name's not Dave!" she giggled, even though her laughter was beginning to subside into the delighted gasps and sighs that follow a good chortle.

The waiter arrived with their pizza, and Libby was finally able to settle down when the waiter asked her, "You okay, ma'am?"

She nodded. "Just had the giggles for a moment, that's all," she explained.

"Okay, well, let me know if I can get you guys anything else, okay?" the waiter said, looking from Sawyer to Libby and back.

"We will. Thanks," Sawyer responded as one last giggle bubbled up out of Libby's throat.

Inhaling a deep breath, she sighed, "Ohhh...I needed a good laugh. And that was a good one. Thanks, Sawyer."

"Well, I'm glad you liked it...and also surprised," Sawyer said.

Libby giggled a little as she took a slice of pizza from the pan between them and put it on her plate. "My name's not Dave. Classic!"

Sawyer took a slice of pizza and skipped putting it on his plate, biting off the skinny point first. Okay, so maybe it had been a back-ended, chicken-crap way to get Libby on a date—asking her if she were hungry and wanted to get a pizza. But it had worked wonders, and now she sat across from him, wiping residual moisture from her eyes and smearing her makeup a bit as she whispered, "My name's not Dave."

She was awesome—more awesome than she was even a moment before, which was incredibly awesome—and Sawyer thoughts were that Libby Meadows just might be the one for him—*the* one, the one he'd end up taking to the altar, to his home, to his bed. In fact, the more he studied her still-amused expression, her sparkling eyes, and her cherry-pink lips, the more Sawyer began to think of Libby as the one woman he never wanted to go another day without seeing.

"So," Sawyer began as Libby took another bite of her pizza, "what's your favorite joke?"

Libby giggled and asked, "You mean *now*? Or before tonight?"

Sawyer chuckled. "Before tonight."

But Libby blushed, shaking her head. "I can't tell you that! It's so lame!"

"Tell me," Sawyer urged, however.

"Okay, but promise me you won't laugh," Libby agreed.

Sawyer smiled and said, "It's a joke, Libby. I'm supposed to laugh."

"But it's not funny, especially compared to 'Hey, Dave,'" she said, a little lingering giggle of amusement at Sawyer's joke tumbling out of her mouth.

"Oh, I'm sure it's funny," he encouraged, however. "Just tell me."

Sighing with resignation, Libby said, "Okay, but you've been warned."

"I have," Sawyer said, winking at her.

"Okay," Libby began, dabbing at her mouth a moment with her napkin. "So there's this preacher, and he likes to make sure he keeps tabs on the little old widow ladies in his congregation, you know?"

"Sounds like a good guy," Sawyer commented.

"Oh yeah! So anyway, over the course of a few weeks, this preacher begins to notice that one of the very elderly widows in his congregation hasn't been attending church. So he's worried, right?"

"Mmm hmmm," Sawyer said, nodding with understanding.

"So the preacher decides he'd better drop in and visit the lady. Her name is Mrs. Smith, by the way," Libby explained.

"That's a pretty unusual name," Sawyer teased.

"I know—almost like Dave, right?" Libby giggled. Inhaling a deep breath, Libby said, "So the preacher heads over to Mrs. Smith's house, knocks on the door, and is really relieved when Mrs. Smith opens the door and greets him. 'Well, hello, Reverend Jones,' Mrs. Smith greeted. 'Come on in. It's so nice to have company, especially you, being that I know how busy you are,' she says."

Sawyer paused in eating his slice of pizza. He placed it on his plate and leaned back in his seat, smiling with amused anticipation.

Instantly Libby felt nervous. Her joke wasn't nearly the caliber of Sawyer's joke—at least not to her. What if Sawyer didn't like it? But figuring it was too late to chicken out, she forged forth.

"So Mrs. Smith led the preacher into the kitchen where they sat down at the table across from one another, and Mrs. Smith began to chatter. And as Reverend Jones sat at the table for over an hour listening to Mrs. Smith's health complaints, stories of her grandchildren, and tales of drama in the neighborhood, he began to feel hungry. When he'd first sat down at the table, he'd noticed that there was a bowl of peanuts its center. So knowing that he was going to be there awhile, listening to the lonely little woman, he asked, 'Mrs. Smith, would you mind if I ate a few of these peanuts?' Being the sweet, kind, grandmotherly woman she was, she said, 'Of course not, Reverend! You eat as many as you want!' With permission given, the preacher reached into the bowl and gathered up a handful of peanuts. Popping them into his mouth one at a time while Mrs. Smith continued to talk, it wasn't long before one handful turned into three handfuls. And before he even realized what he'd done, the preacher saw that the peanut bowl was empty! He'd eaten every last one of the poor old widow lady's peanuts!"

Libby paused as Sawyer sat seemingly transfixed on her. Hoping she didn't screw up the punch line, Libby began to finish the joke.

"Of course the preacher was mortified that he'd been so rude!" she said. "I mean, here was this little old widow woman, obviously on a fixed budget and with many health problems, and he'd sat there and eaten her whole bowl of peanuts. Feeling just terrible about what he'd done, the preacher said, 'Oh, Mrs. Smith, I'm so sorry! I'm afraid I've eaten every peanut in your bowl!' But Mrs. Smith just smiled kindly, reached across the table, and patted the preacher's hand. 'Oh, that's all right, Reverend Jones. They were a gift from my grandson, but I don't really like chocolate-covered peanuts...so I sucked all the chocolate off them just this morning.'"

"Noooo!" Sawyer groaned as he burst into laughter. "Sick! No way!" Libby began to giggle as Sawyer continued to laugh, intermittently saying, "Sick! Oh, sick!"

Even though Sawyer had obviously thought her joke was funny, Libby began to worry that perhaps it was too gross for a girl to tell. Maybe he'd think she was unladylike for telling it. Yet he continued to laugh and moan, "Sick!" for several seconds, appearing to enjoy the joke.

Finally, he inhaled a calming breath and sighed, "That was a good one!"

"Really?" Libby probed.

Sawyer nodded. "Really."

"Whew!" Libby breathed. "After the epic Dave joke, I was afraid mine would totally crash and burn."

"Not at all," he assured her. "Not at all. It was awesome."

Libby's cell began to buzz like a bee trapped in a quart jar. Pulling it out of her purse, she frowned.

"What's wrong?" Sawyer asked.

"It's the alarm company. Something must be wrong at the store," Libby said. Pressing send to accept the call, she answered, "Hello?"

CHAPTER SIX

"Wow," Sawyer mumbled as he and Libby walked across the street to the quilt store. "Two fire engines? But I don't see any smoke."

But Libby smiled, shaking her head with disbelief. "I don't think there's a fire," she giggled. "Look," she said, pointing to where Sue stood talking to a fireman. "I'll bet you a hundred bucks that Sue came back to the shop and set off the alarm system." She giggled again. "She can never remember the code."

"Really? That's too bad…because I think there's a pretty big price tag attached to a fire department response," Sawyer mentioned.

"Oh no, really?" Libby mumbled as her heart sank into her stomach. She really couldn't afford some big bill from the city. She tried not to panic with sudden financial worry as Sue turned and caught sight of her.

"Well? I did it," Sue confessed, brushing tears from her cheeks as Libby and Sawyer approached. "I-I left my tablet in the store when I left today, and I needed it for something, so I came back to the store…and, as usual, panicked when I had to turn off the alarm. I totally spaced the code, and now…now the fire department has had to come out, and I'm an idiot, and everyone knows it!" Throwing herself into Libby's embrace, Sue sniffled, "I'm so sorry, Libby. I'm such a dork! I knew this would happen one day. The alarm system freaks me out. And now they'll probably charge you a million dollars for responding to a call and—"

Libby returned Sue's hug and patted her on the back. "It will be fine," she soothed as she looked past Sue to the handsome fireman her friend had been talking to. She couldn't help but think of Sue's surreal daydreams about falling in love with a fireman—and this guy looked like just the man to fit the ticket. He was tall, attractive, and very impressive looking, decked out in all his firefighter gear.

"Are you the property owner, ma'am?" the man asked when their gazes met.

"Yes, sir," Libby admitted as her stomach began to churn with nausea. Here it came—the no doubt heavy price tag for the fire department response.

"We responded to an active fire alarm at this address," the fireman began to explain. "But interestingly enough, your system didn't notify the police. So I'm thinking there's a glitch somewhere that absolutely needs to be checked out." He grinned at Libby, adding, "So I'm going to have the city waive the response fee for you, on the premise that you agree to have your system thoroughly tested and updated. All right?"

"Oh, thank you so much!" Libby sighed with relief.

"Really?" Sue exclaimed, releasing Libby and turning to face the fireman. "You're willing to do that?"

The tall, dark, and handsome fireman smiled at Sue and answered, "Well...it was an accident, right?"

"Right!" Sue assured him, hopefully. Then with a heavy sigh of relief herself, Sue spontaneously threw her arms around the man's neck and squealed, "Oh, thank you, thank you, you handsome fireman man, you! You have no idea how relieved I am! Thank you!"

The fireman chuckled and returned Sue's hug. "You're welcome, ma'am."

The comforting sound of Sawyer's chuckle drew Libby's attention back to him, and she almost gasped out loud when she was, once more, awestruck by his beyond profound good looks and downright sexiness. The fireman to whom Sue was clinging at the moment was attractive—but even he couldn't compete with Sawyer Delaney's supreme physical appearance.

"I guess you dodged a big financial bullet there," Sawyer said. "I'm sure that's a relief, right?"

"You have no idea," Libby sighed with affirmation.

"Well, I guess I better get home and hit the sack," Sawyer said, stifling a yawn. He grinned at Libby, adding, "Thanks for having dinner with me."

"Thank *you*," Libby responded.

"See you tomorrow," Sawyer said. "We're on the home stretch of your reno...so hang in there with me, okay?"

"Of course," Libby assured him—the thought that she'd hang in there with him forever if he asked her to skipping back and forth through her mind.

"Good night," Sawyer said, turning to leave.

"Good night," Libby called after him.

Once she'd watched Sawyer all the way to his truck, smiling and tossing a wave to him as he drove away, Libby turned back to the near disaster at her back.

She sighed with relief. At least the shop was fine. At least the attractive fireman with whom Sue was blushingly engaged in conversation had cut her a break, saving Libby's financial neck. Libby smiled as she saw the fireman hand Sue his cell phone—bit her lip to keep from giggling out loud with delight as Sue appeared to be entering her cell number into the man's contact list.

"Hmmm," she mumbled to herself. Maybe Sue's intuition where the fireman of *her* dreams was concerned wasn't that far off.

♥

Libby found it impossible to get to sleep at a reasonable hour. Even though she'd kept the store open later than usual and should be beyond very tired, the marvelous experience of being with Sawyer outside of work—the pizza place, the sharing of ridiculously lame jokes, and just merely lingering in his company—had caused Libby's body to flood her with adrenalin. Therefore, even at midnight, Libby found herself up working on Sue's fairy house rather than slumbering peacefully in her warm bed in her little attic room.

She sighed as she spritzed with cool water from a water bottle the soft green creeping oregano and thyme that covered the little house's roof. The moss looked great! She was afraid she'd messed up—hadn't put a deep enough mound of soil in the pie plate she'd secured to the roof weeks before, hadn't watered the plant starts enough, hadn't given it enough sunlight through the small attic window. But now—now Libby smiled as she studied the roof of the fairy house, for the soil-filled pie plate was entirely concealed under a healthy growth of creeping thyme and oregano.

Libby giggled, delighted in knowing how excited Sue would be. A fairy house with a roof of herbs? It was too perfect! The mica-glittered pinecone scales Libby had painstakingly glued around the perimeter of the pie plate looked exactly like perfect little fairy roof shingles, and Libby suddenly realized that, in making the gift for Sue, she'd inadvertently stumbled upon a new little hobby. The fairy house had begun to seem so real to her, just as if fairies really did exist. Libby smiled, imagining that a fairy might actually happen by, fall in love with the miniature home in the attic of the quilt store, and take up residence.

Gently Libby ran her finger along the tiny prisms that hung just inside one of the windows. The tiny prisms had indeed made the perfect valances for the sweet, magical home, and she was glad she'd happened across them in the antique store down the street.

With a heavy sigh, Libby's mind flitted from all the details she still wanted to add to Sue's fairy house and back to her evening with Sawyer.

She swore to herself that pizza had never tasted so good—root beer either! And that "Hey, Dave" joke— hysterical! Libby laughed out loud at the look on Sawyer's face as he'd finished telling her the joke and waited for her reaction. His eyes had been sparkling with anticipation—those beautiful blue, mesmerizing eyes of his. Again Libby sighed with the pleasure of the memory.

She wondered for a moment what would've happened if Sue hadn't set off the store's alarm. Would she and Sawyer have lingered at the pizza place? Shared more stupid jokes? Would he have walked her to the quilt shop door and kissed her good night?

Rolling her eyes, Libby shook her head. "Now you're being just plain ridiculous, Libby Meadows," she said as she set down her spritzing bottle and plopped down in the comfy chair in front of the cold, empty attic fireplace.

She tried not to think of the Sawyer's parting words to her that evening—*We're on the home stretch of your reno.* He might as well have plunged a knife into her heart, for what reason would he have to ever see her again when the renovation was finished?

Still, he'd seemed to think her joke was funny. Maybe he found her more interesting than he did his average female clients.

And then she knew she was overly tired. Thinking she could win over a guy like Sawyer Delaney with a lame—not to mention kind of gross—joke? It was definitely time for bed.

With another heavy sigh—this time a sigh of discouragement and fatigue—Libby silently wished the attic fireplace were safe enough to use. A small crackling fire would be just the thing to relax her at that moment.

Instead, she just rose from her chair, plopped down in her bed, and switched off the little lamp on her nightstand. With any luck, she'd dream about Sawyer Delaney—maybe get that unobtainable good-night kiss she'd wondered about earlier.

Smiling, Libby thought of Sue then—of the handsome fireman who had asked for her phone number. Maybe Sue would get a fireman boyfriend for Christmas, along with the beautiful fairy house Libby had put so much love into building for her. It was a nice thought, but the vision of Sawyer sitting across the table from her in the pizza place was nicer—much nicer.

CHAPTER SEVEN

Over the next few days, Sawyer had a tough time focusing on anything to do with the renovation of Libby Meadows's sewing instruction room. All he could think about was Libby Meadows and how awesome she was.

Of course, he'd thought she was awesome from the moment he'd met her and seen her shop. And of course the more he'd been in her company, the more awesome she seemed. So it wasn't like he hadn't been thinking, well, romantic thoughts where Libby was concerned—even before he'd found the guts to ask her to go for pizza. It was just that, well, after they'd shared stupid jokes and great pizza a couple of nights before, Sawyer hadn't been able to get the steadily growing romantic thoughts of Libby out of his head—not for a moment.

And it wasn't simply because Libby was so pretty or so smart or so capable—or even that there was something uniquely feminine about her. It wasn't the fact that Sawyer found he was fixatedly attracted to her physically or that there seemed to be something refreshingly old-fashioned about her. Nope. Though all of those things were superb and drew Sawyer to Libby like a wasp to root beer, it was the stupid fact that she'd sincerely thought his joke was hilarious that had convinced him to consider a serious pursuit of the girl.

No girl or woman he'd dated had ever thought his "Hey, Dave" joke was funny. Of course, Sawyer thought it was funny from the first time he'd heard it when he was still in high school. He'd roared when he'd first heard it—laughed as hard as Libby had when she'd "gotten it" at the pizza place. Yet no matter how often he told it—no matter how hard he worked to draw listeners in before hitting them with the punch line—no woman had ever laughed. No woman, that is, until Libby Meadows.

And it wasn't courtesy laughter either. Sawyer could spot fake laughter a mile away, and he'd spotted it many times when girls he'd told the joke to laughed and laughed in an effort to please him. Nope. Libby Meadows was the first, and she'd laughed for real.

Sawyer smiled and chuckled a little to himself at the memory of her preacher and bowl of peanuts joke. It was good! He'd laughed at it because it was truly funny; his laughter had been as sincere as hers had been. Libby had drawn Sawyer into the story of the poor old, chatty widow and the well-meaning preacher.

"What's the matter?" one of the guys working on installing a table in one of the sewing stations asked. "You're grinning like an idiot."

Sawyer shook his head, though he couldn't wipe the smile from his face no matter how hard he tried.

"Just thinking of something funny," he answered. "Don't worry about it."

The guy chuckled himself. "Okay, boss. Whatever," he said.

Yep. Libby had liked his "Hey, Dave" joke—and for Sawyer, it was a big deal.

With every passing hour of every day since they'd shared jokes and a pizza, Sawyer had grown more and more certain that Libby Meadows was the woman he'd been searching for his entire adult life. He'd been further assured of it when, after being stumped on one aspect of his current "at-home" renovation project, a light had gone on in his brain and he'd suddenly known exactly how to proceed in order to wrap it up. He knew Libby had been his inspiration where the project was concerned. Still, he couldn't very well tell her she had been. Not without...

"Sawyer. The fireplace guy is here," one of his men announced, startling Sawyer from his Libby thoughts.

Sawyer looked up to see his friend Jeff Martinez step through the plastic drape that separated the reno project from the quilt shop.

"What's up, man?" Jeff asked, striking hands with Sawyer.

"Not much," Sawyer answered.

Of course, that wasn't necessarily true. There was a lot up with Sawyer, but he wasn't about to tell anybody about his mad crush on the quilt shop's owner. Not yet. And besides, he knew it was more than a crush—much, much more.

♥

Libby grinned as she stood working at the cutting table.

"What?" Sue asked. "What's so funny?"

But Libby shook her head and answered, "Oh, nothing." After all, how could she tell her sweet friend Sue that every time she thought of the fireman Sue had been crushing on since she set off the shop's fire alarm two nights before—the fireman whose name was Dave—she wanted to exclaim, "Hey, Dave!" and burst into gut-wrenching laughter?

Sue arched one suspicious eyebrow as she studied Libby a moment. "You're holding something back about your little pizza place escapade with Sawyer the other night, aren't you?" she accused. Her smile faded, and she sighed, adding, "I can't believe I messed up your date with him by setting off that stupid alarm."

"It wasn't a date, and you didn't mess it up," Libby assured her. Libby shrugged and continued, "And besides, the alarm thing was meant to be. After all, how else would you and Dave ever have met?"

"True," Sue agreed. "He's so hot, isn't he?"

Libby bit her lip to keep from giggling, *Hey, Dave!* out loud and nodded. "I've only seen him the one time...but he sure looked handsome to me."

"He texted me off and on for two hours last night, you know," Sue informed her friend.

"Two hours?" Libby exclaimed. "Holy smokes! That's a ton of texts!"

"Yeah," Sue confirmed with a happy sigh.

"What in the heck did you guys text about for two hours?" Libby asked.

Sue shrugged. "Tons of stuff. Favorite restaurants, our families, which schools we went to...you know, the regular kinds of things."

"Does he know any good jokes?" Libby giggled.

Sue's brows wrinkled with puzzlement. "I don't know. I'll have to ask him. Why? Are you thinking about becoming a stand-up comic or something?"

Libby shook her head. "No. Just wondering."

Two hours of texting—wow! Libby wished she could've spent two hours the previous night exchanging text messages with Sawyer. Still, exchanging conversation in person would've been even better! It was weird the way she'd fallen for Sawyer so quickly. He was all she could think about, dream about, and look forward to.

She frowned as, once again, she was painfully aware of the fact that he and his crew were almost finished with the renovation of the instruction area. Three more days and he'd be gone from the quilt shop. Of course, this fact wasn't news to Libby; it's just that she'd spent the last few days trying to figure out how in the world she was going to manage to "stay under his nose" in order to keep his attention as she endeavored to win him.

The familiar ring of the bell on the shop's front door pulled Libby's thoughts from her desperation regarding Sawyer.

She smiled as she saw the tall, dark, and handsome fireman from the false-alarm call step into the shop and begin to glance around. She giggled, thinking how out of place he looked. Oh, he wasn't rigged up in his firefighter stuff—just in jeans, a T-shirt, and a brown barn coat. Still, he wore an expression of not knowing what to do next.

"Why don't you tend to the customer that just walked in, Sue?" Libby suggested, knowing Sue couldn't see the door from where she stood straightening fabric across from Libby.

"Sure," Sue said without pause.

"Yeah...um...I'll go peek in on the renovation, okay?" Libby mumbled as she put down her rotary cutter and hightailed it to the back of the shop.

"Hi, Dave!" she heard Sue exclaim at her back. "What're you doing here?"

Libby couldn't contain her giggles anymore, and as she burst through the protective plastic curtain and into the reno area—as Sawyer turned around and looked at her with an expression of curiosity—Libby whispered, "His name's Dave! The fireman Sue fell in love with the other night. His name's Dave! I haven't told you yet because...because..."

And then it was over. Entirely losing control of her amusement, Libby sputtered, "My name's not Dave!" and burst into such waves of reeling laughter, she had to promptly sit down in the doorway to steady herself.

"What?" one of the workmen asked.

But Sawyer simply strode to her, a dazzling smile of mirth on his handsome face, and asked, "No way. Are you kidding me?"

But Libby shook her head as she continued to laugh. "I'm serious," she choked. "B-but I-I knew I would crack up i-if I tried to tell you before...b-but he's here...in the quilt shop...Dave! Ahhhh ha ha ha ha!"

Libby could not stop laughing. It was nearly as severe a case of the belly laughs as she'd experienced at the pizza place.

Then, as Sawyer also started to laugh, it got worse. Wiping tears from her mirth-filled eyes, Libby could see that Sawyer's crew had all stopped working—were staring at her and Sawyer as if they were sitting there slurping down earthworms.

"Hey, Dave," Sawyer said to Libby through his own laughter. "You're gonna bust an internal organ if you're not careful."

Libby was out of control then, entirely caught up in the moment of hilarity—so caught up, in fact, that she reached out and took hold of the front of Sawyer's shirt, fisting the fabric in both hands.

"His name is Dave!" she laughed. "What are the odds?"

"Did you ask him if he likes peanuts? With or without chocolate?" Sawyer sputtered.

As more laughter wracked Libby's body, she again noticed that the crew was still standing around staring at them. This time, however, they were each wearing a smile and beginning to chuckle.

"Hey," Sawyer said as he caught his breath, "maybe this would be a good time for you to show me that fireplace in the attic you're worried about. Jeff's here to work on the one in here, so I can have him look at that one for you today too." His already broad smile widened as he added, "That way Sue can be alone with…"

"Dave!" Libby choked as she tried to settle down.

"Yeah," Sawyer chuckled as he stood once more. Offering her his hand, he helped her up, saying, "Wow! I can't imagine how easily amused you'd be if you were drunk."

"I don't drink," Libby giggled.

Sawyer chuckled, "Me neither," and they both laughed again.

Turning to look at his crew, Sawyer calmed his laugher, cleared his throat, and said, "I'll be right back, you guys. When Jeff comes down off the roof from checking the chimney, send him up to the attic, will you?"

"You got it, boss," one of the men said. The man paused a moment, looking to one of his crewmen and then back to Sawyer. "But, uh…who's Dave?"

Again Libby began to giggle. She could feel that her giggle would race out of control another time if she didn't escape.

Therefore, as she heard Sawyer answer, "It's a long story," she tightened her grip on his hand and began leading him toward the back stairwell that led to the attic.

By the time they'd reached her bedroom, Libby had regained a measure of her composure.

Exhaling a long sigh and being glad she was able to, she said, "Well…there it is," as she pointed to the fireplace across the room. "Can you just imagine how cozy this room would be if I could have a fire going there sometimes? Especially in winter?"

"I sure can," Sawyer answered.

Libby turned to look at him then. But Sawyer's attention wasn't on the fireplace; rather, he was carefully studying the room.

Libby blushed, realizing she hadn't made her bed that morning before going downstairs.

"Um…it's kind of a mess up here," she said, hurrying to the bed and pulling the covers up over the pillows. "I've got a couple of Christmas projects I'm working on, especially one for Sue—because I don't want her to see it, and since she works in the shop…"

"Is this it?" Sawyer asked, spying the fairy house sitting on the card table in one corner of the room.

"Oh yeah," Libby said, suddenly feeling the excitement of a surge of creative juices hit her as she looked to the fairy house.

"It's, what…a doll house?" Sawyer asked.

"Kind of," Libby answered. "It's a fairy house. You see, Sue loves fairies. She always says she wants to be one. Actually, she used to want to be a spy, but then she started liking fairies so much that she thought she'd rather be a fairy. Of course, in the end she asked me what was wrong with being a fairy spy, and I said nothing…because why can't she be both, right?"

Sawyer chuckled as he hunkered down to peer into the fairy house. "Right," he affirmed. "Wow, it's really detailed. Looks like you're almost finished."

Libby shrugged. "Almost. But I need a front door," she sighed. "And maybe some kind of a water feature, you know?"

"A water feature would be great," Sawyer confirmed. "I mean, fairies and water…don't they kind of go hand in hand?"

Libby wasn't sure whether he was being sarcastic or sincere, but she answered, "Yeah…they do."

"What are you thinking of using for a door?" he asked then.

Libby frowned and smiled, simultaneously curious and delighted. "I-I don't know," she admitted. "I thought of a clock face, but that's so overdone, you know?"

"I didn't...but I do now," Sawyer answered.

"But then...then an idea popped into my head, you know—of something kind of Lord of the Rings style. You know, like the door that leads to the Mines of Moria."

"Yeah, the one they have to utter the Elvish word for 'friend' to open," Sawyer said. "That would look cool as a door to a fairy house."

But Libby stood silent, her mouth gaping open in astonishment that Sawyer had known exactly what she was talking about.

"I can make that for you," Sawyer said, rising to his full height and turning to face her. When Libby simply stood, still staring at him in astonishment, he said, "I mean, if you would like that. I don't have to make it. I mean, if you have some other idea—"

"No, I don't," Libby interrupted, having finally found her voice again. "That would be...well, fabulous! Do you really think you can do it?"

"Absolutely," Sawyer assured her. She watched then as he took his smart phone out of his tool belt and snapped a photo of the fairy house. Then he retrieved a small measuring tape and measured the dimensions of the front of the house.

Typing something into his phone, he then popped it back into his tool belt, turned to Libby, and said, "Consider it done."

Libby smiled, biting her lower lip with delight as all sorts of feelings and sensations of attraction, fascination, approval, admiration, and love began to burst around inside her like internal fireworks. Sawyer was *so* incredible! Not only was he gorgeous, talented, manly, sexy, creative, and funny, he was also helpful and kind too.

She almost did it—almost reached up, took his face between her hands, and kissed him. But she managed not to.

"Now let's have a look at that fireplace, shall we?" he asked.

"We shall," Libby giggled.

She watched as Sawyer studied the outer mortar of the stonework. "Jeff will know better than I will if there's something wrong," he said. "Too bad we didn't think to have him look at this one before he climbed up on the roof to check out the chimney of the other one."

He turned then, looking up to the ceiling and around the room once more. "This really is a cool room. It's not too big, but you can stand up and walk around in it fine. Some of these attic rooms have such low ceilings that you can't stand up straight. Owners have the idea it would be fun to have an attic bedroom but soon find out that it sucks when you can't stand up straight."

Libby glanced around. It was a pretty room—and very cozy.

"I like that the fireplace is in the corner," Sawyer noted. "And the window on the opposing wall of the bed—very inviting. I bet you get a nice view whenever it snows, huh?"

"Yeah, I do," Libby affirmed. "I love to just sit in bed, drink hot chocolate, and read a good book or something. You know…then look up periodically and watch the snow and frost fall. It's really nice when the moon is bright."

"I can imagine," Sawyer said.

Libby smiled and blushed as she watched him surveying the beams in the ceiling. "You're the first boy I've ever let step foot in here, you know."

"Boy?" Sawyer asked, quirking one handsome brow.

Libby giggled. "Boy, man…whatever. They're mostly the same anyway, aren't they?"

Sawyer nodded and returned his attention to the ceiling. "They're exactly the same…on the inside anyway."

"Hey, Sawyer," a man asked as he stepped into the room. "Heard you've got another fireplace up here to be inspected."

"Yeah," Sawyer greeted. "Libby, this is Jeff. Jeff, this is Libby Meadows. She owns the house and shop."

"Nice to meet you," Jeff said, shaking Libby's hand.

"You too," Libby said.

"So she's wondering if this fireplace up here is okay to use," Sawyer said, hunkering down in front of the fireplace.

"I figured there was one up here," Jeff said as he took a flashlight and shone it up into the flue. "I checked out the chimney while I was on the roof, and it looks good. Um…just let me inspect this one a bit, and I'll let you know what needs to be done. All right?"

"Sounds great," Sawyer answered. He turned to look at Libby then, asking, "So? What's the treat in the kitchen for today, hmmm?"

Libby smiled and answered, "Oh, just a little something I like to call homemade toffee."

"Well, let's go then," Sawyer said, taking her hand and heading for the stairs. "You're getting me into some bad habits though…feeding me treats every day like some goat at the zoo."

"They let you feed goats at the zoo?" Libby asked as she descended the stairs behind him. She stumbled a bit, catching herself and preserving her balance by placing a hand on his shoulder a moment.

"You okay?" he asked, stopping and turning around to look at her.

"Yeah," Libby said, blushing with embarrassment. What was wrong with her? She was entirely klutzy and trembly all of a sudden. "I just think my chaka khans are all out of whack or something."

Sawyer smiled, laughing a bit as he asked, "Do you mean your chakras?"

Libby shook her head. "Whatever they're called. You know…those centers of spiritual power or whatever some people think we have."

But Sawyer was gone—lost to laughing so hard himself that he almost stumbled down the stairs.

"My Chaka Khans are all out of whack," he quoted Libby as he continued to laugh all the way to the kitchen.

"What's so funny?" Libby giggled as they sat down at the small kitchen table. Libby took a piece of toffee from the three-tiered china server in the middle of the table. "I know there's a Chaka Khan thing somewhere. Are you sure it's not your Chaka Khans that are supposed to be aligned?"

Still chuckling, Sawyer took a piece of toffee as well. "Chaka Khan is a singer, like, from the '80s. She had that song, 'I Feel for You,' and it starts out with some guy rapping her name."

"Oh yeah!" Libby exclaimed, suddenly remembering. As Sawyer continued to laugh, his beautiful blue eyes so full of amusement they sparkled, Libby said, "Well... I knew it was something like that."

Sawyer couldn't keep from staring at Libby. She was so funny! She made him laugh, and not just because she had a good sense of humor but because he simply felt happy in her company. It was a strange sensation—to be with someone and feel that kind of comfortable happiness.

He was going to have to find the nerve to ask her out again. And hopefully this time, her friend Sue would be too otherwise engaged to set off a false fire alarm.

"Hi, guys," Sue greeted as she entered the room at that very moment, followed by the guy who had been with the fire response team a few nights before.

Sawyer saw Libby catch her breath and try not to laugh as Sue then said, "Sawyer, this is Dave. I don't think you two met the other night."

"Nope," Dave said, offering a hand to Sawyer.

Sawyer stood up, accepted Dave's firm handshake, and couldn't resist greeting, "Hey, Dave. Nice to meet you."

He heard Libby choke then and saw Sue pat her on the back. "You okay, Libs?" Sue asked. "Sheesh! Slow down on the toffee. We can make more."

Sawyer glanced to a red-faced Libby and winked at her with amused understanding. She giggled as she winked back at him, and he knew—Sawyer knew that no matter what, he had to keep himself in Libby Meadows's mind somehow. His reno job for her would be finished in just a matter of days, but he had to find a way to keep her attention. She was the one he wanted— the woman he wanted to laugh with forever! In fact, he wanted her on so many levels he couldn't even sort them out in his brain at the moment. But what he could sort out was that he had to have her.

♥

Anxiety was beginning to creep into Libby's heart and thoughts. Only two days remained; two days and then Sawyer would be finished with her reno job and off to a new one.

Libby wondered if an old lady or a young lady owned the house he was doing a total overhaul on after her shop was finished. Sawyer hadn't mentioned the woman's age when he'd told her about the pending project. Thus, Libby's mind began to wonder whether Sawyer's next renovation project would steal him away from her in more than one way.

Frowning, she turned off the lights in the fairy house, too tired to work on it anymore for one day, and plopped down in her bed.

Closing her eyes, she conjured Sawyer's image in her mind—thought of how amazing he'd looked the night they'd shared a pizza and bad jokes. Then she laughed out loud as she remembered the look on the waiter's face when Sawyer had asked for the check, placed a fifty-dollar bill in the young waiter's hand, and said, "Keep the change, ya filthy animal."

The waiter's eyebrows arched inquisitively. But recognition washed over in the next instant, and he chuckled, "Good one, dude. Thanks."

Libby, on the other hand, had recognized the quote from the classic Christmas movie *Home Alone* immediately and—being that she'd been taking the last swig of her beverage when Sawyer had said it—had nearly spit root beer from her nose as she burst into laughter.

Sawyer told her on their drive back to the quilt shop that he'd always wanted to pull that line on an unsuspecting waiter or waitress but had never had the nerve to try it before. Libby sighed, giggled once more, and snuggled down into her bedding. She was glad Sawyer had pulled the line on the waiter when she'd been present; it was a memory that would crack her up for years.

CHAPTER EIGHT

"Well, by the time you close your shop for the day, your renovation will be complete," Sawyer said as he sat at the little kitchen table across from Libby. Sue had gone out for lunch and brought Sawyer and Libby both a sandwich from the deli in town. Yet no matter how much Libby usually enjoyed her chicken panini, she could do little more than pick at it as she sat talking with Sawyer.

Anyone else in the world would be elated to know that their renovation would shortly be finished, the work crew would be cleared out, and things could settle back down. But not Libby—not when Sawyer would be as long gone as his crew when it was over.

What would she do without being able to see him five or six days a week? How would she ever again manage to enjoy the shop when Sawyer was no longer there?

Sure, the renovated part of the shop would be great—practical as well as another income source when sewing classes began in January. But Libby didn't really care anymore.

As she sat picking at her sandwich, she tried to summon some excitement about the sewing instruction room—or even about the fact that Jeff had done what was necessary to get the fireplace in her attic bedroom cleaned and ready for use. But even the thought of being able to have a fire in the evenings wasn't enough to pull Libby out of her despair as she struggled to think of a way to stay in Sawyer's mind.

"So? Aren't you excited to get me and my guys out of here and get back to your routine?" Sawyer asked.

"Well, your guys, yes…but not you," Libby bravely confessed.

She was relieved when she glanced up to see that, instead of frowning with disapproval by her confession, Sawyer was smiling.

"Ah…well, that's a sweet thing to say," he said. "I guess you're afraid you're going to miss out on some other fantastic, life-altering joke, huh?"

Libby smiled, "Well, there's that too."

"Tell you what," Sawyer began, "how about you meet me for lunch next week? The first few days of a new job are kind of hairy, but by Thursday I should be able to sneak away."

Libby's heart leapt with hope. "I would love it!" she overenthusiastically responded.

"Here," Sawyer began, taking his phone from his shirt pocket. "I'll text you the address of the new project site, and if you can just meet me there Thursday at noon, we'll head out for an hour or so, okay? Think you can talk Sue into manning the guns here while you're gone?"

"Of course," Libby answered. Her heart began to race as she heard her phone beep to inform her Sawyer's text had arrived.

"I thought maybe since you'd finished my sewing room project…that maybe you were finished with me too," Libby ventured. "I mean…isn't that how it usually works? Finish the project, finish the client?"

Sawyer smiled. "Usually. But I hope not in your case."

He winked at her, and again Libby's heart leapt with hope. He liked her; she was sure he did. But did he love her? Could he possibly love her? Did guys' hearts work like girls' did when it came to falling in love? And if they did, did they work as fast as Libby's had when it came to Sawyer?

"And by the way, I made the door for your little fairy house," Sawyer mentioned.

Libby gasped and quietly squealed with delight. "You did? Can I see it?"

"Yep, you sure can," Sawyer answered, "as soon as the reno is all finished and cleaned up and you've approved of it. Then I'll give you your fairy house door."

"I'm so excited!" Libby exclaimed. "Thank you so much, Sawyer!" Rising from the table and going to retrieve her purse from the cupboard she always kept it in while at work, she asked, "How much do I owe you for it? Did it take you a long time?"

"You're kidding, right?" she heard Sawyer ask, however. Turning to look at him, she saw that he was frowning.

"Well…I-I didn't mean for you to do it for free," she stammered.

His frown dissolved, and his smile returned. "Well, I didn't offer to do it for remuneration, Libby. I just wanted to make your dreams come true."

Libby's eyes widened. Had he said what she'd thought he'd said—that he wanted to make her dreams come true? If he had, there sure was one way he could do it—fall in love with her in return!

"I-I mean, I wanted you to have the kind of door you wanted for your little house, you know?" he explained.

Libby smiled—tried not to burst into tears of joy. He was so wonderful! How sweet he was to want to help her with her project for Sue—for free!

"Well, thanks so much, Sawyer," she awkwardly began. "I don't know what to say. You're too sweet."

"Sweet?" he chuckled. "Angel, I haven't been sweet since I was—I don't know—like, old enough to walk."

Libby's heart was so swollen with delight in hope that she felt like it might burst out of her chest.

"And you're really going to make me wait all day to see it?" she asked.

"What? The renovation finale or the fairy house door?" he teased.

"The fairy house door, you brat," she answered.

Sawyer laughed. "Geez, I think you're more excited about your little door than you are about your instruction room being finished."

Libby shrugged. "Well, the instruction room is for business. But the door...the door is for something I've been working on for someone I care for. So it is more exciting to me."

"Well then, I hope it meets up to your expectations," he said. "Now I'm all nervous that it won't be good enough."

"It'll be perfect!" Libby said.

"And how do you know?" he asked.

"Because you made it," Libby confessed, smiling at him as she picked up her sandwich and took a big bite.

Sawyer was encouraged—very encouraged. Maybe Libby *did* like him as much as he liked her—or at least, almost as much. And maybe the little fairy door he'd worried and sweated over for the past two days would win her over completely somehow.

He was tempted to show the door to Libby right away, but he was determined to be patient—to stick to his plan. He'd thought it out long and hard—when and how to give her the door—and he wanted to give it to her alone. First of all, he couldn't risk having Sue accidentally see it. But most of all, Sawyer simply wanted everyone out of the shop—everyone but Libby.

♥

"Hey, Dave," Libby greeted as Dave Miller entered the quilt shop. She was very proud of herself for now being able to address him without cracking up. Considering that Dave and Sue had been inseparable during every free moment they had during the past couple of days, Libby had had a lot of practice.

"Hey, Libby," Dave greeted in return. "Brrrr!" he said, rubbing his hands together. "It's cold out there. Nice and warm in here though."

"And soon to be warmer," Sue flirted as she slipped her arms inside Dave's jacket, pulled herself against him, and met his kiss.

Libby arched one brow. Sue and Dave sure had bonded quickly. For a moment, she was a tad miffed that Sue and Dave were already kissing in public, holding hands, and hugging—and they'd known each other a much shorter time than Libby had known Sawyer.

Yet it was obvious that Dave and Sue were meant for one another. So, Libby figured, what was the point in them making pretenses that they weren't?

"I see all the guys working on the renovation are gone," Dave noted. "Is it finished?"

"It is," Libby answered. "Sawyer said he'd show it to me the moment the store was empty and locked up."

"Well then, let's get out of here, Dave!" Sue giggled. "I want Libby to see what she got for her grandmother's twenty-five grand."

"Wow! Twenty-five grand?" Dave breathed with an impressed whistle for added awe.

Libby nodded. "Yep. But I figure we can recoup that in a few years. And it does add about thirty-five thousand to the value of the home. So I'm okay either way."

Dave nodded, and Sue took his hand, pulling him toward the door. "Come on, Dave, let's get dinner. I'm starving! My taskmaster here forgot to bring me more toffee today."

"Sorry," Libby giggled as Dave opened the door for Sue.

"See you later, Libby," Dave said. "Hope you like your new room."

"She will," Sue answered for her friend. Sue winked at Libby, adding, "Maybe she'll even get up the nerve to break it in properly."

But Libby shook her head. "I'm too tired to sew tonight, Sue. You know that."

Sue rolled her eyes. "I didn't mean for you to break it in by sewing, you dork. I meant, maybe you and Sawyer can break it in by—"

"Shut up!" Libby scolded in a whisper, pushing Sue out the door and then Dave after her. "You two go make out in whatever restaurant booth you choose. Some of us still have to work for a living, you know."

Dave laughed. "See you, Libby."

"Have fun," Libby said as she closed the door, turned the deadbolt to lock, and flipped the sign that hung in the window to display "Closed" to the outside world.

Puffing a heavy sigh of relief, Libby turned, leaned back against the door, and closed her eyes for a moment. It wasn't that she didn't love the shop or love owning and operating it. It was just that sometimes she wished...

"Geez, I thought they'd never leave," Sawyer said as he stepped out from between two rows of fabric shelves.

Libby's breath caught in her throat at the sudden sight of him. He was so handsome; every minute of every day he was handsome. Quickly she studied Sawyer from head to toe, liking the shirt he was wearing, his trademark plaid flannel—and not the baggy flannel shirts but the fitted kind that looked thoroughly masculine and showed off his broad shoulders and chest but proved he was toned and ripped at the stomach too. His jeans were worn—even had a tear at one knee—and his work boots were perfectly scuffed and tattered. All in all, he was absolutely dreamy.

"Are you ready to see your transformed instruction room?" Sawyer asked.

"More than ready," Libby said. "I had a really hard time not peeking in there today, you know."

He smiled. "Oh, I'm sure. Come on. Let's see what you think."

Sawyer was a pretty uptight. Not that he wasn't always uptight when he unveiled a finished renovation or remodel to a client, but he found that, as he led Libby back to the renovation site, he was far more nervous than usual. He did not want her to be disappointed with the renovation in any way. And though he'd done everything the way it was supposed to have been done and even come in under budget by about two grand, he was nervous.

Consequently, his sigh of relief was heavy when Libby walked into the new sewing instruction room in her quilt shop and squealed with obvious and unfeigned delight.

"Wow!" Libby breathed as she stood in the middle of the room, looking around her as if she'd just walked into a ballroom in some castle. "It's…it's unbelievable! It's so beautiful, Sawyer—even better than it looked in your computer rendering! Unreal. Oh, just look at it!" Hurrying to the fireplace where Sawyer had laid and lit a fire an hour before, Libby dropped to her knees before it. Rubbing her hands in front of its warmth, she said, "It's perfect, Sawyer. Look how beautiful everything is! And I *love* this fireplace! It makes the entire room—the entire house—seem cozy and warm and inviting. I think I'm going to start sleeping in here."

Sawyer chuckled, reminding, "What about the one up in your little attic room? Wouldn't you rather sleep up there in front of that one?"

Libby shrugged with being overwhelmed. "I-I don't know. I mean, this room is gorgeous, Sawyer! Look at the sewing stations. They're perfect! And the floor— who knew that floor looked like this underneath that old paint? It's beautiful. Wow…I mean, wow!"

"So you like it then?" he couldn't keep from asking.

Libby stood up, shaking her head in disbelief as she stared at him. "Are you kidding? I knew it would be wonderful, but I had no idea it would look like this!" She paused a moment, frowned a little, and then commented, "Hmmm. It kind of makes the rest of the shop look shabby now."

Sawyer laughed. "No, it doesn't," he countered. "People always think that when they have a reno or remodel done. But it's not true. The rest of the shop is awesome. In fact, the rest of the shop complements this room, you know? Not the other way around."

"Says you," Libby giggled.

Sawyer watched as she walked around the room then, inspecting each sewing station, the newly stained floor, the fresh paint on the walls, the rugs, and the light fixtures. It was apparent that Libby was pleased with the renovation, and again Sawyer exhaled with relief.

"Oh, Sawyer," Libby breathed, returning to stand right in front of him. "I had no idea it would look so wonderful...really. You're amazing! This is...I don't even know what to say."

Sawyer smiled again, kindly reminding, "Well, you did pay me to do this, you know."

"I know," Libby admitted. The sparkle in her eyes was evidence to Sawyer that she was pleased with more than just the results of the renovation: she was pleased with him.

"But," he began. Retrieving a large brown paper grocery sack from the floor just by the door to the sewing room, Sawyer offered it to Libby and said, "You didn't pay me for this. And I think you'll like this even better."

Libby shook her head. "You don't understand. This room...it's perfect! I mean, it's really perfect! I don't see how you could top this."

"Try me," Sawyer dared, this time opening the bag and nodding toward it. "Look inside and take out what's in here."

Goosebumps raced over Libby's arms and legs. In all the overwhelming excitement she'd been bathed in when she stepped into the sewing instruction room, she'd forgotten that Sawyer had told her earlier that he'd made a door for Sue's fairy house.

Her heart was pumping like the engines of the *Titanic* as she peered into the paper bag and then reached into it. The moment her fingers felt the smooth wood of the fairy door, she gasped with excitement, even before she'd seen it. And when she carefully removed it from the bag, tears instantly brimmed in her eyes as she beheld the beautiful door Sawyer had crafted for the fairy house.

"It...it's exactly like the one in the Lord of the Rings—the door to Moria. It's exactly it!" she breathed.

"Well, actually, it's a *bit* smaller," Sawyer teased.

Libby was overwhelmed by how flawless the small door appeared. Not only was it a perfect replica of the door from one of her favorite movie trilogies, but also the attention to detail was incredible. The little wooden door even boasted the familiar vine design carved into it, and the vine seemed to glow bluish-white just as it had in the movie.

"It's beautiful, Sawyer," Libby whispered, unable to find the full strength of her voice. "It's perfect. It's so beautiful! How...how did you make the carved vine glow like this? It's...I can't even..."

"Florescent paint," Sawyer explained. "I mixed blue and white until I thought it looked close to the color the door vines glow in the movie after Gandalf speaks 'friend' in Elvish."

"Are you even kidding me?" Libby squealed with enchantment. "How in the heck do you expect me to part with this? Even for the sake of Sue's Christmas gift?"

Sawyer chuckled. "Oh, I can make another one for you if you really want one."

Libby felt a tear escape one corner of her right eye, but she wasn't about to let go of one side of the door she was holding in her trembling hands in order to brush it away.

"I-I don't know what to say," she breathed. "This is too much. I can't let you just give this to me...for nothing."

"How about you do this for me?" Sawyer said, taking the door from her. "How about we go upstairs and you let me install this on Sue's house before I go? What do you say? I really kind of want to see what it looks like with the house, you know?"

"Of course," Libby agreed, brushing the escaped tear from her cheek. "Let's do it right now. Come on."

She couldn't wait to see the whimsical little door take its place as part of Sue's fairy house! It would be the little house's crowning glory.

As Libby stepped into her bedroom, flipping the switch on the wall to turn on the lamps and overhead light, she couldn't believe Sawyer had done such a kind and thoughtful thing for her.

"Well, here it is," she said, gesturing to the house. "Let's see if it's worthy of such a gorgeous door."

"It's more than worthy," Sawyer chuckled. "I just hope it fits. I made the door frame using the quick measurements I took the other day when I was up here, but I might have to do a little fine-tuning to fit it in just right. And I'll need to glue it, of course."

Libby watched as Sawyer carefully inset the door frame and door into the place.

"There you go," he announced. "Whew! It fits really well. I just need to run out to my truck for some wood glue and—"

"It's *so* perfect," Libby sighed as Sawyer stepped back and admired the little door with her. "I cannot believe how perfect it is! It's, like, so professional and everything."

"I'm glad you like it," Sawyer said, winking at her.

"Like it? I *love* it!" she assured him. "I probably would've just slapped something stupid on there, like a little curtain or something. But your door, it makes the whole thing look…well, it makes it look—"

"Real?" Sawyer suggested.

Libby laughed. "Exactly!"

Sawyer nodded, sighed, and crossed his arms over his broad chest with obvious approval. "It does look good, doesn't it? But remember…it was your concept."

"Maybe, but I could never have made it work," Libby reminded him. Clapping her hands together, she chirped, "Sue is absolutely going to die when she sees this! Just a few more finishing touches, and it'll be finished. Wow, right?"

"Right," Sawyer agreed. "Just do me a favor and don't let it get out that I make doors for fairy houses, you know? I've got a reputation to protect and all," he teased.

Libby laughed. He was cute.

"Wait a minute!" she exclaimed as an idea suddenly popped into her thoughts. "I know what I'm going to do for you, Sawyer Delaney. If you won't let me pay you for this beautiful, perfect little door for Sue's house, then I'm going to make something for you in return."

"You don't have to do anything for—" Sawyer began.

But Libby interrupted, "Come with me," as she took his hand and began leading him out of the room and down the stairs.

"I still need to glue it to the house," he reminded her as he followed.

"I know, I know," she assured him. "But first…"

Fairly dragging Sawyer back downstairs and into the main part of the quilt shop, she led him between two rows of shelves housing bolts of fabric.

"I'm going to make you a quilt!" she announced as she began running her fingers along the bolts of fabric that lined one shelf. "I can't make fairy house doors, and I can't renovate old rooms and houses and stuff. But I can quilt, and I'm going to make you one…as my thanks to you for Sue's door."

"Oh, you don't have to do that, Libby," Sawyer began to argue. "Really. I just wanted to help you out and—"

"Here," Libby began, taking a bolt of winter-themed fabric from the Christmas fabric shelf. "I don't normally work with blue. But for you I think I'll make an exception," she giggled. "And I *do* like this sky blue, kind of light wintry blue." She allowed the bolt of fabric to drop, unwinding a length of about three yards from it as it tumbled to the floor. Looping the length of fabric up over Sawyer's head, she draped it around his broad shoulders.

She smiled, pleased with the way the wintry blue fabric sprinkled with white snowflakes brought out the dazzling blue of his eyes.

"See? This is the perfect color for you!" she said as her excitement about making a quilt for Sawyer grew.

"It complements your eyes. And I'll back it in some soft blue minky so it will keep you warm all winter long." She giggled and added, "You fixed my fireplace and made me a door for Sue's fairy house, so I'll make this quilt in return for those favors. How does that sound?"

Sawyer stared at Libby for a long, very long moment. She was so incredible! So sweet, talented, feminine—strong, yet vulnerable at the same time. And he figured he'd waited just about long enough. He liked her—really liked her—liked her more than he'd ever liked any girl or woman in his entire life. And it seemed to him that the right moment had arrived. They were alone. The lighting was low, the room was warm, and she was smiling at him in a manner that let him know she owned a pretty strong liking for him too. And so, taking hold of the length of the fabric she held in each hand, he whipped the cloth up over his head, then over hers, wrapping it around her back and arms and using it to pull her against him.

Libby's eyes widened, even as she felt her smile broaden and her cheeks blush scarlet. She liked the feel of being held against Sawyer—the sense of the firm muscles of his chest and arms against and around her. His warm breath caressed her forehead as she looked up into the inviting expression of seduction in his simmering blue eyes.

"It's time, you know," Sawyer said in a lowered voice that caused Libby's knees to buckle a bit.

"T-time?" she managed to breathe as his head descended toward hers.

"Yep," he mumbled a moment before his lips pressed hers.

Sawyer's kiss was more perfect than any first kiss in any movie or TV show Libby had ever seen! The first touch of his lips to hers felt somehow supernatural—the way he slowly pressed his mouth to hers, as if he thought she might pull away from him. And then when she didn't—when she stayed there, bound against him by the wintry blue fabric she'd chosen to match his eyes—he kissed her again, more firmly, and she kissed him back.

Sawyer let go of the fabric he'd been using to bind Libby against him, taking her face in his hands. Libby trembled—couldn't breathe as his thumbs settled at her cheekbones, his hands encircling her neck at the back, and his fingers weaving through her hair.

He grinned and mumbled, "I hope that was a good enough first kiss. I was afraid I'd botch it up and—"

"That isn't possible," Libby heard herself interrupt breathlessly.

It seemed to be the encouragement Sawyer needed, and Libby melted against him as he kissed her again—and again. It wasn't long before Libby found herself once more bound in his strong, muscular arms, his mouth open against hers, coaxing a blending of the slow, intense rhythm of his exquisite kisses. The euphoria rising inside Libby made her heart flutter—feel as if it were skipping beats. It frightened her at first, the physical reactions Sawyer was drawing from her body—the powerful emotions he was inspiring in her mind. She felt tears of wonderment and joy, of fear and panic, of desire and desperation gathering in her closed eyes. She loved him! And it was impractical that she loved him! How could she love him? She hardly knew him.

Yet as she wrapped her arms around Sawyer's neck—felt his arms band around her waist—she knew with all that she was that he really was the man of her dreams. And she determined in that moment that she would have him. So what if the renovation was over? It didn't matter. She'd make sure she remained fresh in his mind somehow—because he was the only man she'd ever wanted to keep.

For just a moment, Libby thought maybe she was losing her mind. For just as Sawyer administered a particularly passionate kiss, sending every sense in her body shooting to the stars, the thought crossed her mind that perhaps she could tie him up—keep him for herself that way if she had to. She realized how unsettling her thought of keeping Sawyer captive was, and it caused Libby to pause a moment in returning Sawyer's delicious affections.

He drew back from her a moment, frowning with concern.

"Did I hurt you?" he mumbled.

Libby smiled, touched by his concern. "No," she said. She blushed as she whispered, "You're a really good kisser, you know?"

"Oh, am I?" he asked, tightening his embrace of her.

Blushing three shades darker of crimson, Libby nodded.

"Well, thanks," he chuckled. He winked at her, adding, "But I'll do better when I'm not so nervous. I promise," an instant before his mouth claimed hers again.

As Libby's senses soared to claim residence in resplendence among the stars, she was rendered breathless as Sawyer's mouth worked to prove to her that he was right. For, unbelievably, the next sequence of rapturous kisses he blessed her with was even more sublime than the first.

As the warm, passionate kisses she shared with Sawyer grew in intensity—as the fire burned in the fireplace in the other room, and the autumn rain signaling November's pending arrival began to drip and drop on the sidewalk, lawn, and street outside—Libby Meadows thought of nothing else but Sawyer. Sawyer and his handsome good looks, his incredible sense of humor, the warm, solid contours of his body as he held her, and the fascinating feelings of bliss and breathless euphoria she felt while wrapped in his arms.

CHAPTER NINE

"I'm telling you, Sue," Libby began in a lowered voice, "it was like some made-for-TV romance movie."

"Like Lifetime—television for women?" Sue asked in a whisper.

"More like a Hallmark Channel Christmas movie, you know?" Libby expounded. She sighed, smiled, and continued, "I swear, it was so wonderful! It started out kind of like Richard Armitage and Daniela Denby-Ashe in that BBC miniseries."

"Ooo! *North and South*? I love that kiss! That's my favorite movie kiss of all time!" Sue quietly exclaimed.

Libby glanced over her shoulder to ensure that the several customers in the shop weren't able to hear the conversation she and Sue were having.

"It was exactly like that kiss…the one at the train station at the end," Libby said. "Slow and measured at first, like he was being careful or thought maybe I didn't want him to kiss me or something."

"As if anyone wouldn't want to kiss Sawyer," Sue whispered.

"I know, right?" Libby giggled.

"And so?" Sue urged. "Where did it go from there? From Richard Armitage and Daniela Denby-Ashe? Did it go straight to, like, Antonio Banderas and Catherine Zeta-Jones in *The Mask of Zorro*?"

"No, more like…Ryan Reynolds and Sandra Bullock at the end of *The Proposal*," Libby answered.

"Oooo! That's a great one!" Sue said, nodding with approval.

"I know," Libby sighed. "Only mine with Sawyer was better than that even…way, way, way better. I swear I was dizzy for an hour!"

"Sounds like a one-in-a-million first kiss to me," Mrs. Blair said, suddenly appearing from behind a tall fabric shelf.

Libby blushed as Mrs. Blair stood poker-faced and holding a large handful of fat quarters.

"W-well…it was," Libby confessed.

"I don't doubt it," Mrs. Blair added. She frowned a bit then and asked, "Do you have any fabric of playing cards? Specifically the Queen of Hearts?"

"Um, I actually think we do have some playing cards fabric. Yes," Libby answered. "And I'm pretty sure it has the Queen of Hearts on it."

"I'll take three yards," Mrs. Blair stated, turning her attention to a basket of fat quarters sitting on the corner of the cutting table.

"Well, I'll cut that for you right now, Mrs. Blair," Sue offered.

"Thank you, Sue," Mrs. Blair said.

As Sue hurried toward the back of the shop, Mrs. Blair looked up to Libby once more. With an expression as deadpan as ever, she said, "Snatch that boy up before somebody else does, Libby. He's just plain gorgeous."

Libby blushed again. "Well, I'd love to, Mrs. Blair. But the renovation on my store is finished and—"

"I don't want any excuses," Mrs. Blair interrupted, however. "Snatch him up. Enough said."

"All right," Libby giggled.

"I mean it," Mrs. Blair reiterated.

"Okay," Libby nodded.

Mrs. Blair was such an enigma. She made the most beautiful quilts Libby had ever seen—each one an obvious project filled with love and caring. Yet she hardly ever cracked a smile. It was strange how she managed to remain so guarded.

"I've got it," Sue announced, returning with a bolt of fabric. Plopping it down on the cutting table, she added, "Good thing you thought of it today, Mrs. Blair. It looks like there's maybe only four yards left on the bolt."

"Then give me all four, if you don't mind, Sue," Mrs. Blair instructed.

"You bet," Sue said with a nod.

Libby heard her phone begin to vibrate where it lay on the cutting table. Snatching it up, she smiled and bit her lip to keep from squealing with delight when she saw Sawyer's name on the caller ID.

"It's a text from Sawyer," she breathed.

"Well?" Mrs. Blair asked as she and Sue both stared at Libby expectantly. "Aren't you going to read it?"

"Of course," Libby laughed. Touching her phone's screen, Libby read aloud, "He says, *Decided to start the new project today instead of waiting till Monday…so it looks like we don't have to wait until Thursday to do lunch…if you're free, that is. Can you meet me at 15971 Hidden Creek Ct. at noon?"*

"You can!" Sue exclaimed. "I'll watch the store. Dave can have lunch here with me!"

"Yes, Sue will watch the store," Mrs. Blair interjected. "And take Sawyer some of those treats you have in the kitchen today," she suggested. "It's true what they say about the way to a man's heart being through his stomach, you know."

"Absolutely," Libby said aloud as she answered Sawyer's text.

"This is so exciting," Mrs. Blair said.

Libby looked up, astonished when a slight smile curved the corners of Mrs. Blair's mouth.

"I know," Libby whispered in wonderment and disbelief. Sawyer hadn't just brushed her off after the renovation on her shop was complete. He'd kissed her like she'd never been kissed and had texted her to meet him for lunch the very next day. Mrs. Blair was even smiling a little. That alone was proof that anything was possible.

♥

15971 Hidden Creek Court was an absolutely beautiful Victorian house. It was huge, with a turret, bay windows, everything the cliché Victorian manor should have. And though it was obvious the house needed repair, it was beautiful all the same.

Libby smiled as she saw Sawyer's truck parked in front of the old house. She parked her car across the street, grabbed the brown paper bag full of the treat Mrs. Blair suggested she take with her, and inhaled a deep breath of courage.

As she started across the street, she began to grow nervous, however—nervous over having to face Sawyer for the first time since they'd kissed. Would he have regrets about kissing her? And would they be evident in his demeanor? It was the same old fear every girl had every time she liked a guy, kissed him, and then had to face him. Yet Libby inwardly told herself that Sawyer wouldn't have kissed her the way he had if he didn't truly like her. Furthermore, he wouldn't have called her to meet him for lunch if he didn't truly like her.

Of course, the old-fashioned part of Libby wondered why Sawyer had asked her to meet him, instead of picking her up at the shop or meeting her at a restaurant somewhere in town. But he had started his new reno job three days early, and it was the first day of it, so it stood to reason that it would be difficult for him to get away at *all*. Therefore, Libby surmised that perhaps her meeting him there saved time—enough time that he could slip away for a short lunch.

"Hello, Miss Meadows," a familiar-looking man greeted as Libby stepped up onto the house's front porch.

"Hi," Libby said. She wished she could remember the man's name—because she knew she'd seen him in and out of the renovation project at the quilt shop. Still, Sawyer was pretty much the only person she ever really paid attention to while his crew was at the shop.

"Sawyer's just inside," the man said, smiling at her. "You can just go on in. But I'm warning you that it's already pretty messy in there."

"Thanks," Libby said. "You guys got right to work, I guess, huh?"

"As always," the man said, hurrying past her and out to a truck parked nearby.

Still nervous, Libby stepped through the open front door of the old Victorian home and into chaos.

Workmen were rushing around pulling down walls, ripping up floorboards, and removing debris.

"Wow!" Libby mumbled to herself. She knew then and there that business in her shop would've hit a complete standstill if she'd had a bigger renovation going on than just one room.

"May I help you, ma'am?" a crew member she did not recognize asked.

"Oh, um... I'm looking for Sawyer Delaney," Libby answered.

The man smiled. "Sure. He's right over there talking with the owner of the house," he said, turning to Libby's right and pointing. "You can just go on over there. Just watch your step. We're in demo mode right now."

"Thanks," Libby said as she stared at Sawyer—at the woman he was talking to.

"You bet," the man said as he hurried off.

Libby's heart dropped to the pit of her stomach as she studied the woman Sawyer was in conversation with. She was of average height but not of average body shape. She was built like a supermodel and dressed as though she knew it. Wearing a tight, tapered black skirt hemmed just above her knees, her very tan, very well-sculpted calves drew an onlooker's attention instantly. She wore black platform pumps, complete with ankle straps, and a fitted, shiny purple blouse, unbuttoned scandalously low, accentuating her more-than-ample cleavage. Her long black hair looked like something out of a high-end shampoo commercial, and both her wrists and several of her fingers were dripping with diamonds.

"Holy smokes," Libby mumbled, suddenly feeling wildly underdressed in just her jeans and red sweater.

In fact, as she stood there watching the woman talk to Sawyer—watching her body language, which said nothing less than, "I want you, Sawyer…and I'll do anything to have you"—Libby considered turning and hightailing it before Sawyer saw her. But in that very instant, he looked away from the diamond-bedazzled cleavage queen, catching sight of Libby.

Libby was encouraged at the way a dazzling smile of pleasure spread across Sawyer's handsome face when he spotted her. He motioned to her that she should join him, and even though her self-confidence was shaky at the moment, her feet obeyed his command.

"Hi," Libby greeted as the femme fatale turned and studied her.

"Helena, this is Libby Meadows," Sawyer said to the woman without pause. "Libby, this is Helena Wells. She owns the house."

"Nice to meet you," Libby said, offering a hand to the woman.

"You too," the woman countered, shaking Libby's hand once quickly and studying her from head to toe.

"Libby owns the quilt shop I was telling you about," Sawyer said, speaking to Helena but still smiling at Libby.

"Oh, I see," Helena said, feigning interest.

"We're headed out to lunch," Sawyer began. "So if that's all you have for me right now, I'll let you know when the demo of the downstairs is finished, okay?"

"Sounds perfect," Helena answered. Libby was astonished at how the expression on Helena's face completely transformed when she was looking at Sawyer, as opposed to when she was looking at Libby.

"What's in the bag?" Sawyer asked then, startling Libby from her pondering of Helena Wells.

"Oh! Oh…I…uh…I brought you some turkey turds," she answered, offering the bag to Sawyer.

Accepting the bag, he chuckled, "Thanks…I guess."

"Well, I must say, that's an interesting thing to bring Sawyer for lunch," Helena said, smiling snootily.

Libby blushed, realizing how ridiculous what she said must've sounded. It didn't help that she'd brought the turkey turds in a brown paper lunch sack instead of presenting them in a cute cellophane treat bag the way she usually did.

"Oh…no, no. They're…they're a snack," she stammered. "They're not really turkey turds."

"I would hope not," Helena said.

"Mmm!" Sawyer hummed then. Libby looked to see that while she'd been distracted by Helena, Sawyer had opened the bag and had apparently eaten a turkey turd. "These are awesome! I remember you telling me about these."

"Hmm," Helena sighed. "Well, I guess I'll leave you two to your lunch of…whatever those are. I'll see you later, Sawyer. Yes?"

"Mmm hmm," Sawyer said as he reached into the paper bag and drew out a handful of turkey turds.

"It was nice to meet you," Helena said, forcing a smile as she nodded to Libby.

"You too," Libby fibbed.

She watched as Helena picked her way over and through the demo debris as she headed for the front door in her impractical-for-visiting-a-renovation-site shoes.

"That's some serious cleavage," Libby said aloud.

"That's some serious silicone cleavage," Sawyer added.

Libby smiled, feeling better all at once. *She* had Sawyer's attention now.

"I'm just glad that if I ever get murdered by a serial killer and the coroner can't identify my remains by facial recognition…that they'll be using my dental records to prove my identity and not the serial number on my silicone implants, you know?" Libby said.

Sawyer choked as he simultaneously laughed while trying to swallow a turkey turd. His face turned red as he reached for a bottle of water sitting on a nearby windowsill.

"Are you okay?" Libby asked, patting him on the back. "It wasn't that funny. And I was serious."

"Oh," Sawyer coughed. "I'm sure you were." He took several swigs of water from the bottle and then said, "And she is a piece of work. I'm kind of regretting winning the bid for this project. I can tell she's going to be a pain in the butt." He smiled at Libby then, his gorgeous eyes fairly twinkling with pleasure. "I'm so glad you're here…and that you were willing to come meet me," he said. "It's kind of tacky for me to ask you to meet me for lunch instead of picking you up, but this day is nuts, and I'm lucky I can steal a few minutes at all, you know?"

"I do know," Libby assured him.

"Plus, I have something in my truck I want to show you," Sawyer continued. "I stayed up most of the night working on it."

Folding the top of the turkey turd bag closed, he took her hand and started leading her toward the front door. "You might get mad at me—think I'm too assuming or something—but you kind of said something about wishing you could do, like, a water feature for your thing for Sue, right?"

"Yeah," Libby affirmed as her heart began to swell with excitement.

"Well, I think I figured something out for you...*if* you're interested, that is," Sawyer explained. "I mean, you don't have to incorporate it. But when I got home last night, I was too wound up to go right to sleep, so I fiddled around with this."

He stopped in his tracks as they reached his truck, however, and turned to her, frowning. "I...I was worried all night that you think I'm a total player now," he began. "I mean, it was just a good-night kiss, but...I kind of—"

"If that was just a good-night kiss," Libby interrupted, blushing at the memory of Sawyer kissing her, "then I'd be interested to know what your kisses would be like if you were serious."

"Oh, really?" he said, smiling.

"Really," Libby admitted, astonished at her own daring boldness.

Sawyer tossed the bag of turkey turds into his truck through the open window, and Libby gasped as his hands immediately went to her waist—as he pushed her back against the cab of his pickup.

Leaning toward her, he asked, "Are you game now? In broad daylight?"

"Bring it on, Mr. Contractor Man," Libby giggled.

She had him; Libby Meadows totally had Sawyer wrapped around her little finger. Sawyer wondered if she knew it.

He hadn't slept a wink all night. He'd been too wound up after kissing her, too distracted by the thoughts that were eating at him—thoughts of love, happiness…matrimony. It's why he'd managed to etch out a water feature for the fairy house she was building for her friend—because he'd wanted to do something else for her, something that might get the same reaction from her that the little door had.

"Bring it on?" he chuckled. "Did you actually say bring it on?"

"I did," she admitted, blushing so pink that it made his smile broaden even more.

"Okay," Sawyer mumbled as his mouth began to water at the thought of kissing Libby again. "But just remember…you asked for it."

The kiss that then met Libby's mouth was nearly ferocious—fantastically so! Sawyer was kissing her with no holds barred at all. It wasn't that it was so entirely different than the way he'd kissed her the night before—just more aggressive, more demanding, and Libby didn't mind a bit.

Furthermore, he was kissing her out in the open—in public—in broad daylight! Such a kiss in such a setting was only proof positive that he liked her, that he wasn't embarrassed to be with her. Whatever feelings Sawyer owned for her, they were sincere. His kiss let her know that.

Breaking the seal of their mouths a moment, Sawyer drew back from her a bit, grinned, and asked, "Too much?"

"Nope," Libby managed to answer. She giggled, "And you taste like turkey turds."

"Gee, thanks," Sawyer chuckled.

"It's okay. I *love* turkey turds," she told him.

Sawyer's smile faded a bit. "Think you could love me someday as much as you love turkey turds today?"

"Maybe I already do," Libby whispered.

Sawyer smiled. "Well then, I better keep presenting my bid...until I win, right?"

"Mmm hmmm," Libby hummed as she gazed into the beautiful blue of his eyes. She thought for a moment how perfectly the color of his quilt's fabric matched his beautiful baby blues.

"I mean, nobody has ever loved me more than turkey turds before," he mumbled a moment before he kissed her again—kissed her gently, softly, almost teasingly.

It was too much, his toying with her. Libby wanted Sawyer to kiss her passionately the way he had previously. Therefore, wrapping her arms around his neck and pulling her body flush with his, Libby kissed Sawyer firmly—and with unbridled desire.

His response was exactly what she'd hoped—instantaneous, insistent, and intimate. As every epic movie kiss she'd ever seen flashed through her mind in mere seconds, Libby could not think of one that was as perfectly passionate—as perfectly wonderful—as the one she was enjoying at that moment. As the skillful efforts of Sawyer's warm mouth bathed her in a sort of euphoric intoxication of bliss, Libby doubted that any woman in all the world had ever been kissed with such consummate superiority.

Yet the feelings in her heart were affirmation to Libby that part of the reason she was so lost in paradise in Sawyer's arms—rendered so breathless by the way their mouths blended so perfectly—was because she loved him. Oh, it still sounded ridiculous, even to herself, that she could profess loving a man she hadn't even really dated, but she did. Furthermore, Libby knew that she had to show her hand to him—that for some crazy reason, Sawyer's confidence concerning their relationship was weak. She had to let him know that his confidence should be sure, even if it meant risking heartbreak.

"Way to go, boss!" a man's voice said, rattling Libby from her thoughts of loving and kissing Sawyer.

Relaxing his embrace of her but not releasing her entirely, Sawyer smiled down at Libby as she smiled up at him.

"Hmmm. We might want a more private venue next time," he said.

Libby nodded and breathed, "Agreed."

"For now, let's do lunch, hmm?" Sawyer suggested, ending their embrace. "This project is going to be a stinker," he said, taking her hand and leading her to the passenger's side of his truck. "I'm going to have to put a ton of hours in and do a lot by myself to come in right at my bid. So the next few weeks might be pretty clogged up for me." He opened the passenger's door and helped her into the truck. "But I'll still have time to make this for you," he said, retrieving a piece of paper from the console and handing it to her. "I mean…if you're even interested, that is."

Libby looked at the paper, smiled, and bit her lip with delight as she studied the rendering of a miniature water feature for Sue's fairy house.

"This is what you stayed up working on last night?" she asked.

Sawyer shrugged. "Yeah. But I don't want to step on your creative toes or anything. So if you don't like it, or you're not interested at all…"

Tossing the paper back onto the console, Libby reached out, taking Sawyer's face in her hands and planting a particularly passionate and grateful kiss on his mouth. "I love it!" she exclaimed. "I can't believe you would put so much time and thought into my goofy little project."

Sawyer shrugged again, smiling as he said, "I think it's cool. You've got quite the contractor's eye yourself, you know."

Libby giggled. "Don't you mean I have the eye for quite the contractor?"

"Oh, you're good," Sawyer chuckled. "Keep that up, and we'll never get to have lunch," he said, kissing her mouth quickly before closing the passenger's door of his truck.

Libby sighed as she watched Sawyer walk around the front of the truck on his way to the driver's side. Could Sawyer—that gorgeous, sexy, funny, kind, thoughtful man she was gazing at through the windshield—really like her as much as she was beginning to think he did?

She sighed once more when something deep inside her soul whispered, *Yes!*

CHAPTER TEN

As it turned out, the project for Helena Wells did indeed turn out to be a stinker, as Sawyer had foreseen. In fact, for nearly a week after they'd met for lunch, Libby found that texting and quick phone calls were the only contact she'd had with the man of her dreams. And it was difficult—difficult to keep her confidence up that Sawyer really wanted her.

Still, as it had been for many years, quilting was her solace—her distraction and therapy. Whenever she began to doubt Sawyer's sincere feelings for her, she would work on the quilt she was making for him. It helped. Making a quilt for Sawyer let her think of him constantly yet feel happy and hopeful as she worked.

Of course, Sue said Libby had nothing to worry about.

"Dave is off fighting a forest fire, and I'm not worried," Sue told her one morning when Libby was particularly anxious. "He texts me when he can, and we talk every night. Work is work, Libs. It's something everybody has to do."

"I know," Libby sighed. "But what will I do to keep busy now that I finished the quilt for him?"

Sue shrugged, smiled, and said, "Start one for the first baby you're going to have with him?"

Libby laughed, slapped Sue on the shoulder, and said, "Be serious."

"I am being serious," Sue assured her friend. "The writing is on the wall, Libs. You two are so in love. Anyone can see it. Don't you see it with me and Dave?"

Libby nodded. "Yeah...but that's different. You've been looking for Dave the fireman your entire life."

"And you've been looking for Sawyer, the man of your dreams, for yours," Sue reminded. "Why is it that most people nowadays doubt true love...even when it hits them square in the face? So go. Find some fabric you'd want to see wrapped around a little boy who looks just like Sawyer."

Libby's phone began to vibrate where it sat on the cutting table. Snatching it up quickly, Libby's heart leapt when she saw Sawyer's name on the caller ID.

"Hello?" she answered.

"Hey, baby," Sawyer greeted. At the mere sound of his voice, goose bumps prickled Libby's arms, and butterflies flittered in her stomach.

"Hi! What are you up to?" she said.

"No good, as usual," Sawyer answered. "Hey, I got your text. So my blue-that-you-never-work-with quilt is done, huh?"

"Yeah," Libby affirmed. "I finished it last night."

"Cool! Why don't you bring it over to me this evening?"

"At the project site?" she asked.

"No, to my house," Sawyer corrected. "I'm worn out and need a break. So I should be home about six. And I was thinking that since you work, sleep, eat, and play at that shop of yours, maybe you'd like a change of venue. I'll make dinner for us, okay?"

"Oh, I don't want you to do that," Libby began to argue. "After a long day at the site, why don't you just let me bring dinner to you?"

"Because I want to wow you with my culinary skills," Sawyer answered. "Don't worry. I have it all planned out, and it's an easy meal to fix, okay?"

"Okay...I guess," Libby stammered. "But I feel bad letting you cook when—"

"No arguments," Sawyer said. "I gotta go. Miss Silicone Cleavage just drove up." Libby giggled when she heard Sawyer swear under his breath. "I mean, who wears shoes like that to a renovation site? Oh...and you should see the implants today. If she thinks that's the way to get me to come in under budget, she's an idiot."

Libby giggled, imagining how scandalous Helena Well's desperation to capture Sawyer's attention must look at the moment.

"So my house at six, okay?" Sawyer reiterated. "You need to get out of the shop. I'm at 19275 Sleepy Chestnut Drive. Okay?"

"Okay," Libby said.

"Promise?" Sawyer asked.

"I promise," Libby giggled.

"Good. I'm dying to see you," Sawyer said. "You know...to drink from the nectar of your mouth and stuff."

"Ooo! How poetic," Libby sighed dramatically.

"I try. Okay…see you at six, sexy quilt lady," he said.

"All right, sexy contractor man," Libby laughed.

"Bye," Sawyer said, and Libby pressed end on her phone.

Sue was smiling at Libby, one triumphant brow arched with understanding.

"Sounds like all is well, hmmm?" Sue prodded.

"Sounds like it," Libby admitted. "He thinks I need to get out of the shop, so we're having dinner at his place tonight."

Sue rolled her eyes, shaking her head with frustration. "I say that all the time! But you never listen to me!"

"I do too," Libby corrected her friend. "I went to the mall just yesterday."

"Only because you needed new bras," Sue pointed out. She sighed then and smiled once more. "Well, I'm just glad you're getting out tonight and most of all that you're going to be with Sawyer. You two need to step it up. I'm not getting any younger, you know."

Libby laughed and returned to cutting the strips of fabric she needed.

Yet the goose bumps on her arms and butterflies in her stomach returned every time she even thought of Sawyer for the next hour. She wondered what on earth he would make for their dinner. She wondered what his house would look like. She wondered if he'd like the quilt she'd finished for him. But most of all, she simply could not wait to just be in his company—and hopefully, in his arms.

♥

"19275 Sleepy Chestnut Drive," Libby said as she parked in front of the address Sawyer had given her. She smiled as she studied the house a moment before getting out of her car. It was a beautiful old house that had obviously had been renovated—for it looked too fresh and clean to have stood that way for over one hundred years. It stood out like a beacon among the other old Victorians in the neighborhood. Libby smiled, knowing that Sawyer probably renovated it himself.

She was so excited to see Sawyer, yet so nervous too. Sure, they'd called and texted for the week that they'd been apart. But would he still like her as much as he did the last time she'd seen him in person?

Libby consoled herself, knowing that she still loved him as much as she had a week before—so it stood to reason nothing had changed in Sawyer's mind either.

Libby felt her smile growing wider and wider, and she climbed the steps to the front porch. She giggled with delight when she pushed the doorbell button and heard the familiar Westminster melody chime on the other side.

Almost at once, the door opened to reveal Sawyer standing inside, wearing only a towel around his waist and his hair dripping wet.

"Hi, gorgeous!" he greeted, leaning forward and quickly kissing Libby on the mouth. "I'm running a little behind...so just come on in."

Libby gasped a bit as Sawyer took hold of her arm and pulled her into the house, closing the door behind her.

"I've missed you," he said, taking the large gift bag with his quilt in it that she was holding and setting it down on the floor.

Libby didn't even have a chance to greet him in return—to say hello or "I missed you too"—for she was instantly in his arms where she'd been dreaming of being all week.

Sawyer's kiss was hot and moist—demanding and thirsty somehow. Libby's heart leapt in her chest as she realized her kiss for him was just as thirsty—almost desperate in wanting to be accepted.

She wished she wasn't wearing such a thick sweater, for though her hands were pressed against the warm, smooth contours of his chest, she wished her arms could touch him skin to skin as well.

"Wow!" she breathed as he pulled away from her a bit. "I think you might have missed me almost as much as I missed you."

Sawyer's eyes glistened with emotion as he gazed at her for a long time. He took her face between his hands, kissed her once slowly, lovingly, and mumbled, "I missed you more. I promise you that."

Smiling, he drew away from her and said, "I've got dinner in the oven, and I just need to go dry off better, okay? I'll be right back."

"Okay," Libby said, relieved he still liked her. "What're you making for dinner anyway?" she asked as he turned and strode toward the back of the house.

"My specialty," he called. "Marie Callender's chicken potpies!"

"My favorite!" Libby giggled. She was relieved that Sawyer hadn't slaved over some fancy meal for her. She loved the fact that his specialty was frozen chicken potpie.

Libby had hardly had time to look around the room before Sawyer returned. He entered from the hallway into which he'd only just disappeared, wearing only a pair of jeans and rubbing his wet hair with a towel.

Libby couldn't help but sigh with admiration at the sculpted muscles of his shoulders, arms, chest, and stomach. She'd always figured he looked pretty hot under those flannel shirts he wore, but she'd never imagined he'd look like *that*! In fact, it kind of rattled her a bit—made her nervous.

"You don't have to hurry," she told him. "There's plenty of time. Go ahead and finish getting dressed."

"I am," Sawyer said, reaching into the right front pocket of his jeans and retrieving a rolled-up pair of socks.

Libby giggled as she watched him plop down on the sofa and pull the socks on.

"There," he said, rising to his feet once more and raking his fingers back through his damp hair. "All dressed and ready." He glanced around, his attention settling on the gift bag Libby had brought with her but already forgotten about.

"Now," he said, "is that it? Is that my wintry blue quilt?"

"It is!" Libby exclaimed, remembering the quilt then. "I finished it yesterday. I hope you like it."

"I already know I'll love it," he assured her.

"But you're a guy…and guys aren't into stuff like this the way girls are," she reminded him, picking up the gift bag and offering it to him.

Sawyer smiled his dazzling smile, rubbed his hands together with dramatic excitement, and took the bag from her. Without pause, he opened the bag, pulled the white tissue paper out, tossed it aside, and then removed the quilt.

"Awesome!" he breathed with apparent awe. "Check it out! It's so perfect! Look at these tiny little squares. What are they, like, two inches? Do you have to cut every single square separately? How do you sew these together? It looks so tedious." His smile faded, and he looked at Libby with an expression akin to guilt and said, "I feel sort of bad now…that you went to all this trouble for me."

Libby laughed. "Oh stop," she said, taking the quilt from him. "There are so many tricks that make it go fast. Don't worry." Shaking out the quilt, she turned it so that the minky backing faced her. Maneuvering the quilt to fit around Sawyer's broad shoulders, she asked, "Do you like the minky backing?"

"I do," Sawyer said, taking one corner of the quilt between his fingers and feeling the light blue minky fabric Libby had used to back the quilt. "It's way soft."

"Yeah, I know," Libby agreed. "I usually only back baby quilts with minky, but I thought this would be nice for you…you know, keep you warm in the winter and stuff." She blushed when she looked up to see that Sawyer's attention was on her—entirely on her—and not the quilt.

"Do you like the way the minky feels against your skin?" she asked. "It feels good, huh?"

"It does," Sawyer admitted. "But not as good as you do," he added, pulling her into his arms and wrapping the quilt around them both.

He blessed her with a gloriously delicious kiss and then mumbled, "I've missed you so much," against her mouth.

And it was true. In fact, Sawyer had missed Libby so much during the past week that work had kept him from her that he'd decided days before to throw caution to the wind. Feeling as if he couldn't go one more day without seeing her, talking with her, and holding her in his arms, Sawyer had coaxed Libby to his house on the premise of providing dinner. But there was more to his plan than just two piping-hot chicken potpies. And the way she was responding to him now, both physically and emotionally, buoyed his courage and determination even more.

"I love the quilt, Libby," Sawyer said as he paused in kissing her. Goose bumps suddenly exploded over Libby's arms and legs, for there was a quality to the tone of his voice that she'd never heard before—an alluring, seductive tone that made her skin tingle, her mouth water, and her heart beat faster.

"Wanna see something?" he asked unexpectedly then. Libby was a little dazed. By the intonation of his voice, she'd half expected Sawyer to tell her that he loved her—or in the very least kiss her again. But he hadn't. He'd asked her if she wanted to see something.

"S-sure," she managed to breathe.

Sawyer smiled, kissed her quickly, took her hand, and said, "Okay. Come on."

Draping the quilt over one arm, Sawyer led Libby back into his house—to a bedroom. For a moment, Libby wondered what his intention was. Would she have to tell him that, no matter how much she loved him, she didn't want to even approach a bed with him unless...

"What do you think?" Sawyer asked, jarring her thoughts back to the fact that he was looking around the bedroom. "Do you like it?"

Of course, Libby's attention first fell to the large queen-sized bed that was the focal point of the room. Yet all at once, it hit her—the ambiance and beauty of the room. In fact, as she looked around—studied the padded headboard and beautiful white bedding and quilt, the dimmed lighting, the low-burning fire in the fireplace—as she looked at the refinished chest at the foot of the bed, draped with a chenille throw blanket, the large candle holders and small glass votives on the mantel, all with lit candles burning in them—all at once she realized that she stood in the most beautiful, inviting, cozy, and warm bedroom she had ever seen or even imagined.

"I went with a sort of manila for the base paint and a toasted pecan for the accent walls," Sawyer began. "That way it's warm and bright but still cozy and gives the room a little color, you know?"

"This is beautiful, Sawyer!" Libby breathed in astonishment. She looked at him in awe. "So...so you're an interior decorator too?"

"Oh, hell no!" he said, frowning. But his frown disappeared, and he added, "You just inspire me."

"Me?" Libby asked. "What do you mean?"

"I've had this house for three years," Sawyer began to explain. "I bought it with the intention of flipping it, you know? But after I put so much work into it, I liked it too much to sell it. So I had my sisters help me with putting together the other rooms—though I know enough to do it myself and stuff. But it was fun for them, and they did a good job, right?"

"Yeah," Libby answered—though in truth, she'd been so wowed by Sawyer's shirtless appearance and divine affections that she hadn't really even noticed the décor of his house.

"But when it came to this room—the master bedroom—nothing was coming to me," he continued. "I mean, I'd come up with a theme, or the girls would, but nothing we talked about fit for me in here." He paused, his eyes narrowing as he looked at her. "Not until I met you."

"Me?" Libby asked in a whisper again.

"Yep," Sawyer said. "That first day I met you, I came home, and I was standing in the doorway of this room…and all of a sudden, I thought how great a manila and a pecan paint would complement each other in here. A few days later, I started imagining what kind of bed might appeal to you…and I started to get a vision for what I wanted in here."

Libby smiled up at him. "You're telling me that I was your muse for this room?"

Sawyer chuckled. "I am," he answered. "I know you like that attic room of yours—it's cozy and sweet. But this…"

"It's a big-girl room," Libby offered. "You're saying I need to update my bedroom?" Playfully slapping him on his bare and very muscular chest, Libby said, "You're just trying to hit me up for another renovation job, aren't you? You wanted me to see this so I'd be all, like, dissatisfied with my little attic room and want you to do this to it. You really are a turkey turd."

Sawyer laughed. "No, I really like your attic bedroom," he said. "But you're right. This *is* a big-girl room." He paused, pulling her into his arms and kissing her forehead. "More like a big-girl and a big-boy room though…don't you think? A room that a man and a woman share, you know?"

Libby's smile faded. It was coming now—Sawyer's invitation to sleep with him. And in truth, he was the only man Libby had ever actually wanted to sleep with. Yet she wasn't that kind of girl—the kind of girl that slept with a man she wasn't married to.

Every possible anxiety a woman could ever have about losing the man she'd fallen in love with began to boil inside Libby. And yet she had to tell him—tell him that even though she was so desperately in love with him, she'd always promised herself she'd wait until she was married to…

"I was thinking it could be *our* bed, Libby," Sawyer said—and Libby felt tears well in her eyes, tears of confusion, of fear, of disappointing the man she loved. "Our matrimonial bed," he added then.

"Our matrimonial bed?" Libby whispered. "Matrimonial?"

"Yeah...our matrimonial bed...as in nuptial bed," Sawyer explained. "You do know what matrimonial means, right?"

Libby's heart began to race so quickly it was dizzying. "O-of course," she answered. "When did you turn into Shakespeare though?"

Sawyer shrugged. "I don't know...somewhere between Fifth and Sixth Street." He smiled and winked at her.

"Are you asking me...Sawyer, we haven't even said the three magic words to one another. So I'm imagining this, right?" Libby asked. "You're not asking me to—"

"I love you, Libby," he interrupted. "Ooops...that's four magic words. Forgive me."

"Sawyer," Libby began, still in shock and unable to believe he was asking her to marry him—in a roundabout way.

"I know we haven't known each other very long. Well, at least I'm guessing some people would point that out," he began. "But I do love you. I'm *in* love with you. I want you to marry me. I want that bed to be where we sleep together every night." He paused, grinned, winked at her, and added, "Well, you know...sleep together after, you know...we do other things together."

Libby blushed vermilion with delight. "I love you too," she confessed.

"Also four magic words instead of three," Sawyer said, pulling her into his arms and placing a lingering, moist kiss to her mouth. "So...is that a yes?" he asked.

"No," Libby said, however.

Sawyer straightened his posture, frowning with confusion.

But Libby smiled, took hold of his shoulders, and pushed him down to sit on the beautiful bed. "This is yes!" she said, taking his face between her hands and kissing him with such a kiss that for once *he* was the breathless one.

"Wow," Sawyer breathed when Libby released him at last. "I really like your yeses."

Libby giggled, "I really like when you say 'matrimonial bed.'"

Sawyer smiled. "Matrimonial bed," he said, and Libby kissed him. "Matrimonial bed," he said again, and Libby kissed him. "Matrimonial bed, matrimonial bed, matrimonial bed."

This time when Libby kissed him, Sawyer wrapped his arms around her waist and pulled her down onto the bed with him, ravaging her with hot, impassioned kisses—the sealing kisses of a love that is not only true but everlastingly endless.

EPILOGUE

Libby Delaney stepped back to study the new shop sign. "Hannah's Quilt Shop and Sue's Fairies in the Attic," she read aloud. "I love it! Your sign guy is good, baby," she told her husband.

Sawyer nodded and spun the hammer in his hand into his tool belt as if he were a gunfighter from the old west. "The sign-hanging guy ain't so bad either."

Libby giggled, raised up on her tippy-toes, and kissed Sawyer directly on the mouth. "The sign-hanging guy is sexy too."

Sawyer smiled, took Libby's face between his strong hands, and ground his mouth to hers in a demanding, impassioned kiss.

"Now that's Antonio Banderas and Catherine Zeta-Jones in *The Mask of Zorro*!" Sue exclaimed as she hopped down from the passenger's side of Dave's truck.

Libby rolled her eyes as Sawyer winked at her and put one strong arm around her shoulders.

"The ring has been resized!" Sue exclaimed as she wiggled the fingers of her left hand under Libby's nose.

"It's gorgeous!" Libby said, taking hold of Sue's hand and studying the beautiful engagement ring on her friend's ring finger.

"What's up, man?" Dave greeted Sawyer, shaking his free hand.

"Well…the sign, for one thing," Sawyer answered, nodding toward the shop.

Dave smiled with approval. "It looks great." Putting a strong arm around the shoulders of his fiancé, he added, "And if anybody can sell fairies, it's my little pixie here."

"Really?" Libby teased Sue. "And you make fun of our kissing…when you're a pixie."

Sue winked at her friend, sighed, and said, "You really inspired me with the fairy house, Libs. I swear, Christmas morning was better than any I've had since I found out Santa isn't real."

"Santa isn't real?" Dave asked, feigning being horrified.

Sue playfully smacked his chest. "I love that house, Libby, and it inspires me in so many ways." She shrugged. "I'm sure the shop won't make any money…but it'll be fun, right?"

"Right," Libby confirmed. "If it makes you feel better, I'm giving up all the profit for the quilt shop in order to pay the new employees." She looked up into the face of her handsome husband. "Now I can go back to quilting just for fun…instead of because I have to."

"Yep," Sawyer said. "All you have to do now is use your beautiful body as a quilt to keep me warm at night."

"Oh, come on, dude!" Dave moaned. "I can't compete with that." Dave looked to Sue and asked, "Where does he come up with this stuff?"

Sue giggled, took Dave's hand, and said, "Come on. Let's go see the shop now."

Dave smiled at Sue and followed her lead.

Once they were a ways off, Libby turned, wrapped her arms around Sawyer's waist, and said, "I'm sure glad my daddy hired you to do the renovation in the quilt shop, handsome husband of mine."

"I'm sure glad I bid low enough to win it, beautiful wife of mine," Sawyer said. He paused a moment, seeming to study her face intently. "I keep wondering how I ever made it through life before I met you," he said.

"I'm still wondering how I managed to win the heart of the man of my dreams," Libby sighed.

Sawyer smiled. "It was your reaction to my stupid 'Hey, Dave' joke."

"Really?" Libby giggled.

"Well, that and your turkey turds," Sawyer teased.

"Well, I only married you because you're handsome and sexy," Libby countered.

"You're that shallow?"

"I am," Libby giggled.

"Well, I'm glad then," Sawyer said. "I don't care how I got you. I'm just thankful that I did."

"Me too," Libby said. "I love you, handsome, sexy contractor man."

"And I love you, my little turkey turd," Sawyer breathed as his mouth captured hers in a warm, loving kiss of promise that their life together would be the very essence of dreams.

AUTHOR'S NOTE

And there you have it, my darlings, the third and final novella of 2013—a year that almost beat me under the table! I'm not sure how your 2013 went, but I'm pretty glad to see mine go and start anew with 2014. Now, I don't *think* I'm superstitious, but I never have liked the number thirteen, and 2013 was a really rough year for me, especially where my writing was concerned. These three little novellas you allowed me to do (*A Good-Lookin' Man*, *A Bargained-For Bride*, and *The Man of Her Dreams*) gave me the much-needed respite I longed for this year. And *The Man of Her Dreams* finally got something through my thick skull that badly needed to get through.

You see, once again I failed myself—and in the process nearly failed you! So many people push me to write what they want me to write that every once in a while, I try to write something that does *not* come from my heart. (You know the drill—because I've told you this before. Why is it I never seem to learn and stay learned in this regard, hmmm?) Unfortunately, I fell into the same rotten trap when I first started writing *The Man of Her Dreams*. I tried to write something that I was forcing rather than writing from my heart and venues of inspiration.

But then, something magnificent happened. Shannon came to visit! That's right, Shannon—good ol' turkey-turd-making Shannon, the extremely gifted chef, caterer, Party Posse member, and wonderful bosom friend of mine! Yep, Shannon came to visit me, and it changed everything where *The Man of Her Dreams* was concerned.

Sure, Kevin and my daughter, Sandy, had told me to quit stressing about *The Man of Her Dreams*—to listen to my heart and not the pressure from others and write what I felt inspired to write. Even my editor kindly suggested that the story felt forced. But it wasn't until Shannon came to visit and I turned off my computer for a few days, letting go of the story—it wasn't until Shannon came and we began talking fabric and found this fabulous quilt store in Corrales that I had never known was there before—that I was really able to focus and really *feel* this story unfolding.

One evening during Shannon's visit, as she and Kevin sat with me in our family room, listing off the reasons they thought I was unhappy with this book— the biggest reason that popped up was that, once again, I was trying to force myself to include storylines, characters, and situations that didn't make me happy. It was then that I suddenly shook off that weird funk I get into sometimes, and a light went off in my brain. So guess what? I entirely trashed my first draft of *The Man of Her Dreams*! I literally started over, keeping only the main characters' names and the original dedication to Shannon—at least at first.

As I started anew, I felt wholly liberated and really began to enjoy the story. After all, this was me—purely my own heart's desires where the romance between Sawyer and Libby was concerned. Whew! Another disaster averted just in time.

Why do we do this to ourselves? Why do we let other people plant doubt in our minds and hearts when we know the right thing to do, huh? And why do we keep falling into the same trap over and over again?

I think a lot of it is stress, especially when your job is on the line. We all have so much on our minds, so much drama going on all the time, that we just don't have our emotional immunities built up. And we totally need our emotional immunities to be strong and in vast reserve. My advice on how to keep our emotional immunities healthy and ready for the next round of battle with emotional flu bugs? Unplugging! And I don't just mean from technological devices but from anything that tends to suck us dry. We need time to simply sit and think—to ponder—to watch the lights on the Christmas tree blink and just (in the profound words of one Neil Diamond) "Be." We need to take more morning walks out away from the noise and traffic if we can. We need to spend more time playing games with friends and laughing. We need more funny jokes that allow us to laugh the way "Hey, Dave!" allowed Libby (and me) to laugh. We need to cuddle babies and just hold them for an hour while they sleep in our arms and take more trips to DQ for Peanut Buster Parfaits. We need to give our brains time to detox and revitalize. We do *not* do that enough these days.

I swear to you now that if I had given my brain some detox time—some downtime to watch a couple of lighthearted Hallmark Channel movies—I would not have detoured off on that forced first attempt at writing *The Man of Her Dreams*. So here's my new plan: each time before beginning a new book, I'm going to unwind a while. I'm just going to watch Hallmark movies and make cookies and cuddle my grandbabies while they're sleeping (and while they're not). I'm going to drink hot chocolate if I want (even if it is packed with sugar and calories) and leaf through the American Girl catalog that keeps coming in the mail (even though I've never ordered an American Girl anything). I'm going to doze off on the couch for an hour, laugh with my friend Sandy on the phone, and just "Be." When my brain is all relaxed and my emotional immunities recharged, only then will I start the next story that's been dominating my dreams, okay?

It's my solemn promise to you that this is absolutely the last time I will have to go through rehab for starting books with forced elements that I've been bullied into. I'm healed, at last! When I look back at this year and think of the things I've finally stood up to, recognized, and overcome, I don't feel quite so bad about myself as I did last January. And that's always a good thing!

And now that that muddy water is under the bridge for the very last time, get ready for trivia snippets from *The Man of Her Dreams*! I think you'll find the real-life story of the night I heard "Hey, Dave" quite a lot more embarrassing for me than it was for Libby. Furthermore, you'll love the recipes I've included for my mom's hot chocolate and Shannon's turkey turds!

As always, I hope you enjoyed this quick little story of romance—that it made you smile and feel ready to soldier on through another demanding day. Just be sure to keep your emotional immunities up. I recommend turkey turds and a Hallmark Channel movie. ☺

Yours,
Marcia Lynn McClure

The Man of Her Dreams Trivia Snippets

Snippet #1: Attic Rooms and Fairy Houses—I've always liked the idea of attic bedrooms. You know, cozy little hideaways with slanted ceilings, a fireplace, and a cozy bed, a place where one can escape, sit and read in privacy, maybe write in a journal, or just do nothing. So it's not so unexpected that I would include an attic bedroom in Libby's house. Furthermore, though I've always loved the idea of fairies—always thought it would be fun if they really existed and always wanted a pretty little fairy doll or figurine collection—it wasn't until my friend Amy (a.k.a. "Aimes the Would-Be Spy") mentioned to me that she loved fairies as well that I discovered "fairy houses." Well, I'd sort of discovered them years ago in the movie *A Fairy Tale*, based on the true story of the Cottingley Fairies (*love* that whole thing, and I find the photographs the girls took and the story that followed wildly intriguing). But it wasn't until I started shopping around for something fun to send

Aimes for her birthday that I discovered the tradition of building fairy houses, especially on the coast of Maine. And now, as I myself have become interested in building fairy houses, the inspiration for Sue's fairy house that Libby constructs *is* in honor of my darling friend "Aimes the Would-Be Spy." If you've ever read my book *The Whispered Kiss*, you'll note that part of the book dedication is to Amy. At that time, Aimes's greatest ambition was to "someday be a spy." Yet some months ago, I received an e-mail from Aimes, in which she stated, "I haven't given up on being a spy, but I have decided I want to be a fairy also. Maybe I will be a fairy spy! I haven't really started collecting fairy stuff, but I like anything fairy. The fascination with fairies started when I was in Washington and bought a fairy for my garden. There is a lady that works in our office that is into fairies, and so my fascination and interest has been growing!" Thus, for Christmas this year, I gifted Aimes several fairy-themed items that I gathered from the four corners of the earth (otherwise known as Amazon.com). Because once I find out someone likes a thing, like fairies as Amy does, that person and the corresponding thing they like are forever linked in my mind. Just ask Abby who likes owls, Kathleen who collects penguins, or "Aimes the Would-Be Fairy Spy" who now (like it or not) will be collecting fairies.

Snippet #2: Sawyer Delaney—There actually *is* a cuter little story behind our hero Sawyer Delaney's name. You see, I've always liked the name Sawyer. I suppose it comes from my lifelong adoration of Mark Twain's character, Huckleberry Finn. I mean, even though I liked Huckleberry far, far, far more than Tom Sawyer, I've always considered Sawyer a cool name. In addition, I've always thought of Sawyer as a boy's name—that is until about eleven years ago when my cousin and his wife named their adorable little girl Sawyer. At that point, my little girl cousin named Sawyer became the reason I had put off using the name Sawyer as a hero in my books. But when I began writing *The Man of Her Dreams*, Sawyer just fit so perfectly for, well, you know, Sawyer. So I decided to go ahead and go with my gut. Unfortunately, however, a last name for Sawyer didn't come to me as naturally as his first name did. Thus, I tried various names, but none of them stuck. Well, one morning as I was struggling with coming up with Sawyer's last name, I wandered into our bedroom to wake Kevin up. (You see, I'm a lark—an early riser—and I'm usually up-and-at-'em between 4:30 and 5:30 a.m. On the other hand, Kevin is a night owl—goes to bed about 2 a.m. and gets up between 8 and 9 a.m.)

I lay down on the bed next to Kevin about 6 a.m., and finding that he was already awake, I ventured, "So I've named the hero in this book Sawyer but I can't think of a last name for him. Any ideas?"

Kevin paused for a moment and then casually suggested, "How about Delaney? Sawyer Delaney?" Now this may not seem very amusing to you…at least not yet. But maybe when I mention that my little cousin Sawyer, well, she has an older sister named—you guessed it—Delaney! Delaney and Sawyer, my two little girl cousins, inspired the name for the hero of this book, Sawyer Delaney. Who woulda thunk it, huh? And kudos to Kevin, right?

Snippet #3—My Mom's Hot Chocolate: The following recipe is the jotted-down version of how my mom made hot chocolate all the years I was growing up. She always did it by estimating the amounts of the ingredients, and so do I. But I figured it might be better to give you a more precise version, so I made myself a giant mugful of it today and wrote down the amount of each ingredient for ya. Now, *I* love this recipe, but it is very, very rich and not for the faint of heart. In fact, I remember one holiday season when my mom relished a serving of this deliciousness every night before bed. She gained 10 pounds before she figured out what was putting the weight on her tiny little 110-pound body. P.S. One more thing: if you're having trouble getting to sleep, this is a great treat to enjoy before bed. It will knock you out cold!

My Mom's Hot Chocolate

Makes 1¾ cups of hot cocoa—About 2 servings

Ingredients
1 scant tablespoon cocoa
3 scant tablespoons sugar
Dash of salt (optional)
2 drops to ⅛ teaspoon pure vanilla extract
¼ cup water
1¼ cup evaporated milk

1. In a large mug, mix cocoa, sugar, salt, and vanilla.
2. Add ¼ cup water, and mix well.
3. Heat in microwave for 35 seconds.
4. Remove from microwave and stir until sugar and cocoa are dissolved.
5. Add 1¼ cup evaporated milk and stir.
6. Heat in microwave for 1 minute. (If evaporated milk was refrigerated before use, a second heating cycle of 30 seconds or so will be necessary.)
7. Stir, mixing well. Taste and add a bit more sugar if necessary (don't burn your tongue!).
8. Relax and enjoy!

Snippet #4: The Pitfalls of Mercy Dates—Ahhh, the infamous mercy date, something most of us have experienced at one time or the other and on one side of the coin or the other. Either we've been pursued and hunted by someone and caved in and agreed to go out, or we've been the hunter and pursuer and driven someone nuts. Either way, it almost always turns out badly. I learned this the hard way when I was a senior in high school. A boy who was a fun friend in one class kept asking me out. I liked him as a friend, but had absolutely no attraction to him otherwise and certainly didn't want to encourage him. Yet he was so persistent, and I felt like a jerk for not accepting his offers to take me out. So one day I did accept his offer, and I'll never forget how awful *I* was! He wasn't a very cute guy, you see, and I was older than him too. And what I remember is just being so embarrassed to be with him on a date. How shallow was I, right? Ugh! It was pretty out of character for me to be like that; in fact, I was usually the girl who was determined to make the awkward guy feel great! But this date with my friend had disaster written all over it before it even began. For one thing, he was a terrible driver! I was literally in fear for my life as he drove us to the movie theater. I remember praying over and over all the way there that I would make it home safely. I won't go on about it any longer and just wrap it up by saying it was one of the worst decisions I'd ever made in my life to that point. I sure learned my lesson, and today I pray that sweet boy didn't know how shallow I was. Although I did stay friends with the boy throughout high school, I never accepted another date from him, no matter how many times he asked. I'd learned my lesson in being kind—and mercy dates are never kind. Someone always gets hurt.

Snippet #5: Shannon's Shirtless Men Pillowcases and Mrs. Blair—So a few years ago, my friend to whom this book is dedicated, Shannon, brought me the funniest gift—a gift that would turn out to be quite iconic at any future book signing events. I was having lunch with my darling Party Posse friends (I *love* those girls! Where would I be without them?), and Shannon announces that she's made something fun for me. Well, lo and behold, she pulls out these pillowcases she'd made— pillowcases she'd made out of a fabric print that was shirtless cowboys! It was hysterical! The Posse members and I fell in love with Shannon's pillowcases, simply because they were just too fun! Thereafter, whenever the Marcia Lynn McClure Party Posse puts on an event, a few of Shannon's shirtless-guy pillowcases are always on the list of things given away to lucky ticket holders who attend. And by now, you've guessed it, Mrs. Blair appears in the story, simply as a venue to remind my Party Posse of how much fun we have with those fabulous pillowcases Shannon makes!

Snippet #6: The Real-Life Story of the Night I Heard "Hey, Dave!"—Blade Mueller and I had a long history, almost before our history began. It started in the third and fourth grades—our mutual attraction. What followed were years and years of on-again, off-again crushes and romance—opening in the fourth grade when he presented me with a beautiful, jewel-bedazzled engagement ring. (I still wonder where he got it—because it was totally legit! An adult woman's ring with so many tiny little diamond and pink rhinestones that it must've cost a mint, even for the fact that it was bedazzled with faux jewels, you know? I've often wondered over the years if he didn't pilfer it from his mom.) I believe Blade was my first legitimate kiss (out in the tall grass behind his house in, like, sixth grade) and possibly my second kiss (in the garage at my house—until his little brother sprayed aerosol Spray 'n' Wash in my eyes and I had to go "flush with water" for several minutes). In middle school, Blade and his family moved from Albuquerque to another small town in New Mexico and didn't return until Blade had graduated from high school there.

Thus, knowing that Blade left as a gangly middle-schooler and returned in 1983 six-foot two and better-looking than ever, walking straight back into my heart after a five- or six-year absence lets you know how much in puppy love we'd been off and on since elementary school. And in that long-ago summer of 1983, my romance with Blade was quite different than it ever had been before. (First of all, there were no little brothers to spray aerosols at us.)

That summer, I was working in downtown Albuquerque as a receptionist at a law firm, and Blade was working at his uncle's auto shop just a few blocks away. Therefore, we often met for lunch. In late July or August of that same summer, Blade also bought tickets to the Journey concert and invited me to go with him. It was incredible! (I mean, you know how much I loved Steve Perry and Journey back then. In fact, the Journey T-shirt Blade bought for me at the concert became quite the item! I took it to college and nearly wore it out. My sister would then sneak it to wear to school. And twenty years after that concert Blade and I enjoyed so much, my daughter loved wearing that same Journey T-shirt to school. After all, it was vintage by then and even cooler than it had been originally).

Yep, Blade and I had the best summer in 1983. Of course, the Journey concert was the peak of it all. We even had quite the romantic interlude afterward—sitting out in my front yard under the warm summer moonlight, with a million stars twinkling overhead— until about 5 a.m. when I had to catch a Greyhound bus down at the bus station in order to travel up a couple of states for a youth conference I was attending that began the next day.

However, it was our date to see the movie *War Games* and go for pizza afterward that stands out in my mind most vividly. Yep, that was one of the best dates I ever went on—if not *the* best! One reason was because I was so comfortable with Blade. I mean, we weren't in love at that point—just in really, really, really deep like. Neither one of us was probably aware of that fact then; it's something I realized later.

Anyway, Blade and I were going out. He picked me up, and we drove to the theater and sat in seats about midway down. I can still see it—to this day—at this moment, I can see us. He was sitting to my left, and we were scrunched down in our seats so that we could talk privately. It was just comfortable and fun, you know?

We had a while before the movie was scheduled to start, so we just enjoyed entertaining conversation.

Then, unexpectedly, Blade says, "Want to hear a joke?"

I'm always up for a good joke, so I said, "Sure!"

You guessed it—what followed was the "Hey, Dave!" joke!

Now here's the thing. I know that joke isn't all that funny (at least when I tell it). In fact, I've never been able to get anyone to think it's even mildly entertaining. But the way Blade told it that night—perfection! When he delivered the punch line of, "My name's not Dave!" I thought I was going to blow up laughing so hard. I mean, he really drew me in, you know? I was all invested in this poor guy's life. I *must* be forgetting something important in the telling of the story, because no one ever thinks it's as funny as I did that night. In fact, for years and years and years, and even now, whenever, "My name's not Dave!" pops into my thoughts, I giggle. Seriously, it was that good, the way

Blade told it that night anyway. What a great joke! (P.S. I know I didn't do it justice in this book either. Sorry.)

Well, when the movie was over, it was time for pizza. Now, you have to understand that way back in 1983 pizza was a big deal! For one thing, it was expensive. And for another, it wasn't delivered to your door the way it is now—or even the way it was later that year. Nope, back then you went to the pizza parlor, sat down, and ordered your very expensive pizza, and once it arrived at your table piping hot and smelling like heaven, you relished every bite.

So the movie was over, I was still silently giggling to myself here and there at "Hey, Dave!" and Blade and I ordered our pizza. Man, oh man, it was good too! Delicious!

It's important that I point out that I was wearing a hot-pink blouse with black pinstripes that night. The blouse was a totally cool '80s blouse, made out of something similar to taffeta. It was bright and shiny and "dry-clean only." Wanna know why it was "dry-clean only?" Well, because any moisture that happened to get on the blouse—such as perspiration, water, or *melted ice*—left not only a big, dark, very obvious wet spot but also a ring when the wet spot dried!

Now, even though I weighed much, much, much less back then than I do now, in 1983 my height had already put me in the habit of resting my "bosoms" on a tabletop whenever I was seated at a table and leaning forward in conversation. Normally, this wasn't so bad—leaving nothing more than a few smudges of pencil lead on my bosoms from leaning on my desk or something, right. Nothing a squirt of the ol' Spray 'n' Wash couldn't handle—at least on cotton. But on hot-pink taffeta…

So there we sat, leaning across the table, eating delectable pizza, and drinking root beer. Periodically, I'd use my straw to coax a piece of ice out of my glass to suck on, right? And, though I do *not* remember dropping a piece of ice, it is certain that I did—for as Blade and I sat up straight in our booth seats, preparing to leave—*whoomp*, there it was! Somehow I'd dropped a piece of ice on the table and then, unaware, rested my bosoms right on it while leaning forward to talk to Blade and eat pizza!

I promise you that the Bat Signal in a clear, cloudless sky was less visible than the fifty-cent-piece-sized wet spot perfectly placed (horrifically placed) right over my left (sorry, but I have to say the word) *nipple*! Ahhhh! It was horrifying! There might as well have been a flashing red light placed there!

To this day, I can't remember who noticed it first—though I'm pretty sure it was Blade. Either way, I'm still amazed that I didn't drop dead of embarrassment—or that Blade didn't. What happened was actually pretty funny. Maybe I'd just been through so many other embarrassing moments by then, or maybe I was just more mature, but whatever the reason, Blade and I simply had a good, nearly uncontrollable laugh as we left the restaurant—me with my arms folded across my chest.

Okay, maybe it doesn't sound so bad to you—but it was! I'd never been a lactating new mother at that time, mind you, but I sure looked like one—and in hot pink! (I never wore that shirt again, by the way.)

Anyway, there you have the inspiration for Sawyer and Libby's first date to get pizza. Looking back, I wonder what Blade Mueller remembers most about that night, if he remembers it at all. Does he remember how much I loved his, "Hey, Dave!" joke? Or does he remember the rogue piece of ice, smack over the nipple incident of 1983?

Snippet #7: The Fairy House Door—Yes, I *am* a Lord of the Rings movie fan! Die-hard, forever fan! Thus, the door to Sue's fairy house.

Snippet #8: Are Turkey Turds Real?—Yes, Virginia, they are! Turkey turds are a very real (and very delicious) treat! About two years ago, my friend Shannon (to whom this book is dedicated) gave me a couple of freezer bags full of something she called turkey turds. As she handed me the bag (a treat she'd made for Kevin and I to share on our drive home from doing some author events), she said something to the effect of, "Here are some turkey turds I made. I thought you'd like to nibble on them during your drive home." I was more than mildly amused at the idea of nibbling on turkey turds, though Kevin was a bit hesitant, being that the turkey turds Shannon had made really did look just like authentic turkey turds—you know, from authentic turkeys. Well, a very few miles down the road, I opened one of the freezer bags full of turkey turds, and *wham*! The moment the first turkey turd touched my tongue, I was hooked! Even more impressive was that Kevin was hooked too! And he usually isn't tempted by anything sweet, other than ice cream. Kevin and I devoured that bag of turkey turds so fast you would've had to have replayed it in super-slow mode in order to even know they'd ever existed. We also kept thinking, "Why, oh why, did we give the other freezer bag full of turkey turds to our kids to share in the car they were following us in?" Yep, they're that good!

Since being introduced to turkey turds by my darling Shannon, I have done my best to spread the addiction. In fact, I made a big batch of turkey turds while another friend was visiting later that same year, and I made the mistake of setting the giant bowl of fresh turkey turds in her lap while we were watching a movie. After about half an hour of raving about how delicious they were, we turned the lights on to find that my friend had eaten almost the whole bowl full—probably the equivalent to four regular-sized bags of Cheetos!

Now, to show you just how wonderful, kind, caring, and selfless Shannon is, she's letting me put her turkey turds recipe in this snippet! Can you imagine? Yep, we're spreading the love with this one! You may have seen similar recipes for this scrumptious little treat, but Shannon adds a secret ingredient that makes all the difference in the world in the flavor and experience of her turkey turds. So thanks to Shannon, we can all distribute freezer bags full of turkey turds to our friends and loved ones this year!

"Shannon's Turkey Turds"

Ingredients
2 cups brown sugar
1 cup butter
½ cup maple syrup
1 teaspoon baking soda
1 teaspoon vanilla
2 3½-ounce bags of Chester's Butter-Flavored Puffcorn

1. In a saucepan, combine brown sugar, butter, and maple syrup. Stirring constantly, heat to boiling, and boil for 5 minutes. Remove from heat, and add baking soda and vanilla.

2. Preheat oven to 300 degrees. Dump puffcorns into a large bowl (large enough that you have room to stir them well), and pour mixture over puffcorns. Mix well, coating corn puffs as thoroughly as possible.

3. Once puffcorns are thoroughly coated, pour them into a large roasting pan. Bake at 300 for 10 minutes, and then stir well and bake for another 10 minutes.

4. Spread turkey turds on waxed paper and allow to cool, but do mix them periodically. These are inexplicably delicious!

Snippet #8: "Keep the Change, Ya Filthy Animal"— I've always, always wanted to have the nerve to hand a big tip to a waiter or waitress and say, "Keep the change, ya filthy animal," the famous quote from the *Angels with Filthy Souls* movie Kevin McAllister watches when he's home alone in the movie *Home Alone*. But I've always been too afraid that said waiter or waitress won't get it, you know? And waiting on tables at restaurants is a hard enough job without whacked-out *Home Alone* fans trying to be funny. So Sawyer did it for me.

Snippet #9: In Regard to Breast Implant Surgery—Did I ever tell you about my friend who always wanted to have breast implant surgery? She always claimed her chest was actually concave, that she had no bosoms whatsoever. Therefore, her goal in life was to have the surgery, for she knew that it would be a much-needed lift (no pun intended) to her otherwise low self-esteem and self-consciousness. Well, she started saving up, and she was getting a pretty good nest egg toward her surgery. But then, as fate would have it, the opportunity came for her, her husband, and their children to move from New Mexico to the one state in which she'd always wanted to live—Oregon. Therefore, she called me one day with a dilemma. You see, the family could afford to move to Oregon only if my friend were willing to give up her savings that she'd worked so hard on, hoping to afford breast augmentation, and use it for the move.

"And so," she said to me on the phone that day, "apparently it's Oregon or bust."

Ah ha ha ha ha! No, I'm not kidding!

In the end, she decided that she wanted Oregon more than bosoms, and so the family used her bosom money to move to Oregon.

The reason I mention this at all is that Helena Well's silicone cleavage—well, it's kind of my tribute to my dear friend who never did get her bosoms. But she *did* make it to Oregon!

And now, enjoy the first chapter of
TAKE A WALK WITH ME
by Marcia Lynn McClure.

CHAPTER ONE

Cozy Robbins exhaled a long sigh. She was tired, and her eyelids felt droopy. Yawning, she leaned back in her chair, running her fingers up through her long hair and stretching her arms over her head. Glancing to the clock on the wall, Cozy wondered how she had managed to finish thirty more Christmas tree ornaments before midnight. Of course, these were only tiny clay mice tucked snuggly beneath hand-stitched quilts in walnut shell cradles. They weren't as tedious to make as the hinged walnut halves with Christmas tree and fireplace scenes depicted inside them. Still, they were far more difficult to craft than the simple gold-paint-dipped walnuts with ribbon loops Cozy also made.

She shook her head, wondering how in the world she had gotten herself into taking so many orders again. Things certainly had escalated in the past five years. It seemed difficult to fathom—the hundreds of ornament orders she still needed to fill—when just five years previous, she'd been astonished at having sold sixty ornaments total.

Cozy closed her eyes and sighed once more in thinking back to the November she had been sixteen—to the first series of finely crafted walnut ornaments she'd made to sell. She'd wanted to purchase something nice for her Grandma Robbins for Christmas that year—a beautiful set of bookends she'd seen in a specialty shop, knights in armor posed in kissing princesses. The moment she'd seen the bookends, she'd known they were just what her grandmother had been looking for to adorn the bookshelf in her entryway. But they were costly, priced at nearly three hundred dollars for the set.

At sixteen, three hundred dollars was hard to come by, especially when it was to be spent on only one gift. Still, the bookends were ideal for her grandmother, and Cozy had begun to ponder ways she could make the three hundred dollars—for in truth, how often did the perfect Christmas gift present itself? Ironically, it had been her Grandma Robbins who had suggested Cozy make and sell her charming walnut Christmas tree ornaments. Though she had no idea why Cozy wanted to acquire three hundred dollars, Dottie Robbins (the very person for whom Cozy was inspired to earn the money) suggested her granddaughter sell the delicately crafted Christmas ornaments.

Cozy's grandmother had always adored Cozy's walnut ornaments. In fact, Cozy had begun making them for her grandmother in the first place. She'd been ten years old and wanting to give her grandma something special. She had seen a plastic walnut ornament in a bin at a second-hand store. The plastic half walnut shell had a little plastic mouse nestled in it, nibbling on a piece of cheese and wearing a Santa hat. Cozy thought it was the most adorable thing she had ever seen and begged her mother for fifty cents to purchase it. The little Christmas tree ornament had fast become Cozy's greatest treasure. To some, it may not have been worth even the fifty cents, but to Cozy it was priceless.

Consequently, Cozy had spent an entire afternoon cracking open walnuts and hollowing out the insides until she found just the perfect shells to make her own ornaments. She used gray molding clay to form little mouse heads. Carefully she'd painted tiny black eyes and noses and nestled them into the shells. With old fabric scraps her mother had given her, she then cut and stitched tiny quilt tops, tucking them snugly around the little clay mice. She had figured out how to fashion a way to hang the ornaments by using lengths of gold thread so that the walnut cradle would hang perfectly from any Christmas tree branch.

Cozy had presented these first walnut ornaments to her grandmother on Christmas Eve that year. Dottie Robbins had been delighted to literal tears, claiming Cozy's walnut cradle ornaments were the most wonderful gift she'd ever received. After that Christmas, Cozy worked on improving her ornaments. Every year she presented her grandma with several new walnut ornaments, and Dottie was always just as excited as she had been the day she received the first ones. Gradually, Cozy began to diversify her craft. She hollowed out walnuts by the hundreds. Some she would glue back together, painting them gold and adding a red ribbon at the top to provide a means of hanging it. Her favorite ornaments, however, were the ones with two walnut halves hinged together. When opened, they revealed either a miniature nativity scene or a miniature Christmas scene—one half having a tiny Christmas tree with gifts at its base nestled within and the other boasting a little fireplace, complete with stockings hanging from the mantel. These required a lot more work with clay and detailed painting, but they were Cozy's favorites. Yes, her walnut ornaments had become quite popular around town.

As Cozy tucked one special ornament into a small white box with her gold embossed logo (two robins sitting on a holly branch, their heads lovingly pressed together and the trade name *Cozy Robbins* beneath them) stamped on the top, she wished she could see the look on the girl's face when her boyfriend handed her the ornament and told her to open it. The young man had contacted Cozy about a making a specialty ornament. She had agreed to do it, of course—to hide the diamond solitaire engagement ring inside a gold, red-velvet-lined walnut.

"How romantic!" she sighed, smiling and setting the box aside. She glanced at the clock again, even though she already knew the time. She had to get to bed. Her shift started early, and she didn't want to be too tired.

Exhaling another sigh of weariness, Cozy rose from her chair. Two more semesters and she'd have her degree. Surely she could stop waiting tables at the café then. She glanced at the table covered with Christmas ornaments made from walnuts. She could hardly believe she'd managed to pay for every one of her winter college semesters with the proceeds from selling such a little thing. Oh, it was a ton of work—no doubt it was. Still, the whole concept that walnuts could pay for a college education was almost unfathomable.

Reaching over to the electrical outlet nearby, Cozy unplugged the Christmas lights she'd strewn over the ceiling of the basement. She blew out the pumpkin-spice-scented candle on the table and turned off the old stereo, and the soothing music she listened to while working at night was silenced. The basement room that had seemed so warm and inviting a moment before was dark and cold and quiet now. Cozy smiled, amazed at what a few Christmas lights, an aromatic fragrance, and some soothing music could do to brighten up a dark space.

Hurrying up the stairs, Cozy brushed her teeth, threw on a pair of pajamas, and fell into bed. Morning and the early birds who frequented the café would arrive all too soon. Still, Cozy smiled, for a vision of her grandmother's delight at seeing the new ornaments Cozy had made for her lingered in her mind like a comforting dream. Grandma Dottie always brightened Cozy's day. Therefore, Cozy decided to look on waitressing at the café the next morning as a means to a happy end. She hadn't seen her grandma in almost a week and could hardly wait to leave work and drive over to see her the next day.

She loved spending time with her Grandma Robbins—she always had. As far back as Cozy could remember, her grandmother had been one of the most wonderful things in the world to her. Cozy knew Dottie Robbins's affection, influence, and love had helped shape her life—still did shape it—and she could not imagine an existence without her.

With one final sigh, Cozy's mind wandered toward sleep with the tender memory of being two or three years old and her grandmother pushing her in the old swing that still hung, faded and worn, from one T-bar under the clothesline in Dottie Robbins's backyard. In her mind, she could still hear her grandma singing "The Teddy Bears' Picnic" as she gently pushed the swing and then attached a sheet to the clothesline with a clothespin from her apron pocket. Cozy could almost feel the warm breeze on her face as it billowed the clean white sheets hanging on the line—still hear the birds as they twittered around her grandmother's bird feeder—still smell the sweet perfume of freshly mown grass...

❦

"Cozy!"

Cozy turned to see Mindy hurrying after her.

"Have you got any extra ornaments?" Mindy asked, rushing toward Cozy's car. "I know I already put my order in, but I forgot a couple of people."

Though the question rather deflated her enthusiasm, Cozy smiled at her friend. A sale was a sale and meant more money for tuition—whether or not she was getting tired of walnuts. She felt a giggle tickle her throat as Mindy characteristically puffed at the blond bangs on her forehead.

"Sure," Cozy answered with more enthusiasm than she really felt. "How many were you wanting? I'm still making them right now...so if there's something special you want..."

"I want four nestled mice cradle ones and four hinged nativities, if it doesn't stress you out too much," Mindy answered. Again she puffed at her bangs. Cozy felt her heart lighten even for having to make eight more last-minute ornaments. Mindy was too sweet—too kind and supportive of Cozy as a friend and a customer—for Cozy to deny her anything.

"Eight? That's a couple?" Cozy asked.

Mindy shrugged. "I guess it's more like a few, right?"

"I guess," Cozy giggled.

"Do you mind?" Mindy ventured. "I know you like to have the orders before now."

"I don't mind at all," Cozy answered with a just little less than perfect honesty. "Are you sure you want to spend that much though? That's eighty bucks...I mean, forty."

"I'm sure," Mindy confirmed. "Can I bring some cash tomorrow?"

"Yeah...but why don't you just make it twenty."

"Cozy Robbins," Mindy scolded. "You have got to quit underselling your stuff! Your ornaments are so charming, and they're hard to make, I'm sure. Ten dollars apiece is a steal, and you should quit cutting your friends and family that crazy five-dollar discount on each one. I'm paying eighty."

"No," Cozy argued. She hated charging her friends and family anything at all, and she certainly wasn't going to let them pay full price. "I'll take twenty...or I won't make them for you."

"Cozy," Mindy scolded.

Cozy sighed, relenting, "Okay then. Forty. Dang! That's like four movies at the theatre…or a new pair of shoes…or—"

"Stop it!" Mindy giggled. "They're worth it, Cozy. They are the most adorable things in the world! People are willing to pay for adorable…so let them. Okay?"

"Okay." Cozy shook her head, still unable to believe someone would drop even a dime on Christmas ornaments made out of walnuts. Her smile for Mindy broadened—for if there was one thing her ornament sales had taught her, it was who her true friends were. So many people asked for freebies because they knew Cozy personally. Yet she found that her real friends understood she made the ornaments as a supplement to her income. Her genuine friends never tried to take advantage of her or haggle her down. It was a valuable life lesson to her—and an example she followed in her own dealings with friends. Still, she absolutely loathed letting them pay for anything. But she knew it was important to Mindy that she take some kind of remuneration.

"Good. I'll bring cash tomorrow," Mindy said, smiling.

"If you must…but it's still a waste of forty bucks," Cozy giggled.

"Shut up!" Mindy laughed. "I have to get back…so have fun with your grandma. I know she'll love the new ornaments."

"Thanks," Cozy said. Nodding toward the café, she added, "And good luck tonight."

Mindy's eyebrows arched with understanding. "Thanks. I hate the dinner shift."

"Sorry."

Mindy shrugged. "I'm fine. Just thankful to have the job, you know?"

"I do know," Cozy agreed.

"Okay then…have fun."

"You too."

Cozy watched Mindy return to the café, silently reminded herself how glad she was not to have the dinner shift, and felt guilty.

Opening her car door, Cozy turned when she heard a familiar rustle. The leaves of the cottonwoods were quickly changing from green to gold as autumn descended in its full beauty. She paused a moment, for she had promised herself a long time before that she would always, always take the time to watch the leaves transform in the fall—that she would never, never be too busy with ornaments or work or anything else to miss it.

She lingered in watching the breath of the breeze cause the green and yellow leaves to tremble. The air was crisp and refreshing. The moment soothed Cozy even more than punching out from work had, and she felt her smile broaden.

She got into her car, turned the key in the ignition, and pulled out of the café parking lot. She hoped her grandmother had planned meatloaf and mashed potatoes for supper; she loved her grandma's meatloaf and mashed potatoes. In fact, it was the only meatloaf she really liked. There was something special about her grandma's meatloaf—something nostalgic and old-fashioned—and Cozy's mouth began to water as she drove toward the bridge.

"Over the river and through the cottonwoods," she said aloud to herself. With a delighted giggle of anticipation, she began to hum the familiar words to the song that had prompted her thoughts. Secretly, she loved the fact she had to drive over the river and through the cottonwoods to get to her grandmother's house. Cozy thought of the way her mother used to sing the song every time the family traveled to her grandmother's house when she was a child. It was a wonderful little sentiment—a wonderful memory—and it added another measure of joy to her already happy mood.

❦

"Grandma? I'm here," Cozy called as she closed the front door behind her. "Grandma?"

"In here, sweet pea!" Dottie Robbins called from the other room.

Cozy smiled. Her grandmother's voice was like music. How she loved the happy sound of it.

Setting a basket of new walnut ornaments on the entryway table, Cozy hurried toward the kitchen. She could already smell the meatloaf cooking. Supper would be delicious—as was always the case at her grandma's house.

"Hi, Grandma," Cozy said as she entered the kitchen to see her grandmother peering out through one of the windows.

"My angel!" Dottie said, turning from the window and drawing Cozy into a warm embrace. Cozy smiled as the light fragrance of rose perfume tickled her nostrils. "It seems a coon's age since you've been here."

"I know," Cozy agreed. "I'm sorry. I've just been so busy that I—"

"I know, sweet pea," Dottie said. "But you're here now, and we're going to have a wonderful evening!"

"As always," Cozy said as her grandma released her.

"I've got a meatloaf in the oven, and…" Dottie began, clasping her hands together just like an excited child, "and I'm hoping you brought me some new ornaments today."

"I certainly did." She frowned as uncertainty washed over her. "I hope you like them this year. I did a few things differently and—"

"I'll love them, and you know it!" Dottie laughed.

Cozy studied her grandmother for a moment—her smiling, twinkling blue eyes, the sweet little wrinkles on her face. Her grandmother's hair had once been a dark, dark chocolate-brown like Cozy's, but it had faded to a beautiful snowy white. Cozy thought it was very becoming and hoped her hair would do the same—but not until she was in her sixties like her grandmother was.

Dottie Robbins glanced to the window she'd been gazing through when Cozy had entered the room. Cozy frowned, curious—wondering what could be so interesting.

"What are you looking at, Grandma?" Cozy asked, going to the window.

"The handsomest hunk of burning love I've seen in a long, long time…that's what," Dottie sighed.

"What?" Cozy giggled. She looked out the window to see an elderly man raking leaves in the backyard next door. "Who's that?" she asked.

"My new hunk of burning love neighbor, that's who," Dottie answered.

"Grandma!" Cozy exclaimed. She laughed. Her grandma was so funny sometimes.

"Well, just look at him!" Dottie said, nodding toward the window. "Isn't he just the dreamiest man ever?"

Cozy gazed out the window once more, giggling as she studied the man. He was tall, silver-haired, and as tan as leather. He wore an old barn jacket and worn-out work boots, and Cozy shrugged, thinking he was indeed a striking figure. She couldn't see his face very clearly, but it was obvious he was a hard worker.

"He moved in last week," Dottie offered, "and I've been watching out my windows every day since. He's got the deepest blue eyes. They just set my heart to palpitating!"

"Grandma...you have a crush?" Cozy teased.

Dottie smiled. "Of course, angel! Wouldn't you if you were my age?"

Cozy's smile faded just a little. When her Grandpa Robbins had passed away seven years before, the family feared Dottie might follow him too soon. A deep, aching depression and loneliness had overtaken her grandmother. It was one reason Cozy had begun to visit her at least once a week—to remind Dottie Robbins how loved she was and to cheer her up. It had taken a couple of years for Dottie to return to some semblance of the woman she'd been before her husband's death. Therefore, it was surprising to see her puppy-eyed over another man.

Even so, Cozy felt her heart leap a little. It was wonderful to see her grandmother so rosy-cheeked and excited. She thought for a moment that her grandma looked like a schoolgirl in that moment, blushing with the excitement of a new boy in the neighborhood.

"Well? What's his name?" she asked her grandmother.

Dottie's smile broadened. "Buckly Bryant...Buck for short," she answered. "Isn't that a wonderful name? It sounds like he just rode into town on a white horse, doesn't it?"

"Yeah, it does," Cozy agreed. "So you've met him then?"

"Of course! I went over and introduced myself last Thursday while the movers were moving his things in. I swear, Cozy...he put my heart to hammering like a woodpecker!"

Cozy giggled as her grandma placed a hand over her heart as if it were still hammering. "Well, good! You need a little romance and excitement in your life, Grandma."

"Do I?"

Cozy nodded, noting the pink that rose to her grandma's cheeks. "Of course! Everyone needs it...and you deserve it too."

Dottie glanced out the window once more—rather longingly—and exhaled a wistful sigh. "He is a tall drink of water, isn't he?"

"Yes, he is," Cozy agreed.

With one final sigh, Dottie turned her attention from the window and her handsome neighbor in his backyard to Cozy. "Well, as I said...I've got the meatloaf in the oven. We can put the potatoes on in about an hour. Meanwhile…" She paused, gleeful anticipation twinkling in her blue eyes. "Meanwhile, show me what you've made this year. I've been so excited to see the new ornaments! I could hardly wait. I almost snuck down to the basement last time I was at your house…but your father stopped me."

Cozy laughed. "Oh, Dad's very protective about my ornaments," she explained. "He doesn't want the surprise ruined for anyone. Still, it's not like they're really any different than the ones I've made in the past."

"Cosette Robbins!" Dottie scolded. "That is simply not true. Why…every year they're different. And I don't know how you manage it…but they keep getting better and better."

"You're my grandma. You have to say that," Cozy said.

"I am your grandma…but I'm sincere in my compliments."

Cozy nodded. "Okay then, come and see what you think."

Dottie rubbed her hands together like a silent-movie villain as Cozy went to the entryway and retrieved the basket of ornaments she'd brought. Returning to the kitchen, she set the basket in the center of the table.

"Oh, I can hardly stand it. The anticipation is glorious!" Dottie exclaimed, sitting down in a chair and pulling the basket to her.

Cozy sat down next to her and tried to hide her amusement in her grandma's delight. She bit her lip, unable to hide her relief and pleasure as her grandma gasped when she opened the first little white box.

"Oh, Cozy. It's adorable! Simply too adorable for words," Dottie exclaimed as she carefully took the small walnut cradle, complete with a mouse reading a tiny copy of "The Night Before Christmas" and tucked beneath a red flannel quilt. A miniature oil lamp on one edge of the walnut cradle and a tiny green nightcap for the mouse completed the scene.

Again Dottie gasped with awe. "I *love* it, Cozy. Oh, I love it!" She picked up her reading glasses from the old lazy Susan that had lived in the center of her kitchen table for as long as Cozy could remember. "Oh, look at that! How did you ever paint the title on that book? And look at the little lamp. Oh, Cozy…I *love* it! I just *love* it. Just look at the stitching on the quilt! Oh, however do you manage to make the stitches so small? Oh, I love it. I absolutely love it!"

Cozy smiled. She could tell when her grandma was sincere in her compliments, and she was certainly sincere. She felt relieved—and elated.

"Well, if you like that one, then you should freak out over this one," Cozy said, taking another box from the basket and handing it to her grandmother.

Dottie paused and inspected the *Cozy Robbins* logo embossed on the box's lid. "I have to admit, I'm kind of proud of myself for thinking of this—the two little birds…the two cozy robins."

Dottie giggled, and Cozy said, "You should be. It was very clever."

"And memorable," Dottie added. "People remember it. Something this cute sticks in their minds."

"I know…and I'm glad."

Dottie reached out, cupping Cozy's cheek with one hand. "I love you, sweet pea," she said.

"I love you too, Grandma," Cozy said, taking her grandma's hand in her own and squeezing it for a moment. "Now…see if you like the others."

"Oh, I know I will, sweetheart. I know I will."

Cozy sighed. She loved her grandmother so much! What would she ever do without her?

"So? Where did he move from?" Cozy asked, dipping a forkful of mashed potatoes into the melted butter puddle at the center of the far too large helping of mashed potatoes her grandmother had plopped on her plate.

"The east side," Dottie answered. "He said he'd always wanted to live in the valley, along the river. So when the opportunity presented itself, he moved. He lost his wife a few years ago and was having trouble with the blues, as he put it. He's a retired firefighter."

"Wow! A real-life hero, huh?" Cozy asked, smiling.

"Well, he sure looks the part!" Dottie giggled. "I swear, Cozy…I had butterflies in my stomach the whole time he was talking to me! For a minute there, I felt like I was seventeen and he was the proverbial captain of the football team, you know?"

"I can imagine," Cozy said. She smiled as she took a bite of meatloaf.

"What?" Dottie asked.

Cozy shrugged. "Nothing. I was just thinking."

"Thinking what? I know that look. You're up to mischief, Cozy."

Cozy sighed. "I was just thinking that maybe Mr. Buckly Bryant will whisk you away on some romantic adventure. He looks like he's a good kisser."

"Oh, for pity's sake, Cozy!" Dottie laughed. "The things you come up with. What an outlandish thing to say!"

But Cozy saw the merry twinkle in her grandmother's blue eyes. She wished for a moment that her own eyes were blue. Cozy had her father's hazel eyes, but she'd always wished they'd been blue. Still, she contented herself with being glad she had her grandmother's chocolate hair.

"It's not outlandish," Cozy argued. "He's a hunk of burning love. You said so yourself. And you're ravishing. You'd make a perfect couple."

"Now stop that teasing, Cozy Robbins," Dottie playfully scolded. "You're being ridiculous, and you know it."

"No, I'm not, Grandma," Cozy argued. She paused a moment and then suggested, "You should bake him some of your banana nut bread and take it over—you know, as a housewarming, welcome-to-the-neighborhood sort of thing. Once he tastes your banana nut bread, you'll have him eating out of the palm of your hand."

Dottie smiled and laughed a little. "You know, maybe I should." She shrugged. "I mean, it *would* be the neighborly thing to do."

"It would be," Cozy encouraged. "And I still say he looks like a good kisser!"

"Cozy Robbins!" Dottie scolded. "Shame on you."

Still, Cozy could tell by the blush rising to her grandma's cheeks that she was thinking the same thing.

"Grandma…I love your meatloaf and mashed potatoes," Cozy sighed.

"Thank you, darling." Dottie placed a warm palm to Cozy's cheek. Nodding to the small blue bowl of green beans on the table, she added, "And those are the last of the green beans from my garden for this year."

"They're delicious," Cozy assured her.

"I know," Dottie said, shrugging her shoulder with delighted pride.

Cozy laughed. She felt as if she were caught in a moment of perfect wonder. Sitting at her grandmother's table enjoying a supper of meatloaf, mashed potatoes, and green beans—it was peaceful, warm, comfortable, and relaxing. The rhythmic ticking of the clock on the wall was soothing, and Cozy sighed. It was a moment to cherish, as was every moment spent with her grandmother, and Cozy consciously committed it to memory.

"I suppose women my age do still kiss, don't they?" Dottie asked.

"Of course they do, Grandma," Cozy exclaimed. "If Grandpa were still here…wouldn't you still be kissing him?"

Dottie smiled a melancholy smile and whispered, "Yes. Definitely yes."

Cozy's heart ached, knowing she may have caused her grandmother pain in provoking a memory of loss. "I'm sorry, Grandma. I only meant—"

"I know, darling," Dottie soothed, smiling. "And you're right." Her smile broadened. "Mr. Buckly Bryant does look like a good kisser."

Cozy giggled and took another bite of butter-slathered mashed potatoes. The cuckoo clock in the hallway announced six o'clock, and Cozy was glad the time was ticking by slowly. There would always be ornaments to make, bills to pay, and things to do, but there wouldn't always be time with her grandma. At least she had that priority straight.

"So are you dating anyone yet, honey?" Dottie asked.

Cozy sighed. "I went out with Tristan Plummer last Friday."

"And how did that go?"

Cozy shrugged. "Okay, I guess. But he's so…so…"

"Soft?" Dottie suggested.

"Exactly!" Cozy confirmed. "Like I might expect to see him coming out of the nail salon with a new manicure or something. His hands are so…you know…"

"Soft," Dottie reiterated.

Cozy nodded. "Yeah."

Dottie sighed. "I worry for you girls today, sweet pea. Masculinity itself is under attack, it seems. Society is forcing men from their natural, instinctive path. Men weren't made to be cooped up in a cubicle unable to do anything physical. They were made to be hunter-gatherers, to work hard in body and mind. It's hard for men these days…for women too. Femininity isn't what it used to be either."

Cozy sighed, for she agreed—wholeheartedly. Yet what could be done about it? Society was what it was, and it certainly wasn't going to let up.

"Well, Mr. Buckly Bryant looks masculine enough," Cozy offered.

"Yes, he does," Dottie whispered with a wink.

"You definitely need to whip up a batch of your banana nut bread, Grandma," Cozy giggled.

"I think you might be right, sweet pea."

"Of course I'm right," Cozy said, dipping another forkful of mashed potatoes into the butter well on her plate.

❦

Later that night, Cozy sat in her bed, writing in her journal while tucked comfortably beneath a soft flannel quilt. She had had a productive day and a tranquil, wonderful evening with her grandmother. She was tired but truly content.

Still, it seemed contentment never lasted long. Cozy's bedroom door suddenly burst open, and the peaceful moment was shattered as her younger sister Ashley literally hopped into the room.

"Can I borrow your pink sweater for tomorrow, Cozy?" Ashley asked.

Cozy sighed, wishing she could have afforded to live on campus for one more semester at least. The lack of privacy in living at home was so frustrating sometimes. Still, she loved her home—and her family— even if her little brothers and sisters did drive her nuts.

"I guess so, Ash," Cozy answered.

Ashley smiled and hurried to Cozy's closet.

"Why are you in bed so early?" Ashley asked. "It's only ten."

"Why are you up so late? It's already ten," Cozy teased.

Ashley smiled. "I'm totally nervous, that's why! I don't think I'm gonna sleep a wink tonight!"

"Why's that?" Cozy asked—even though she already suspected there was boy at the core of Ashley's discontent.

"Because Kaylee *swears* she heard Braden Lewis telling a friend that Dylan Hill is going to ask me to the winter formal tomorrow night. And if you want to know the truth…I'm totally freaking out!"

"Because you want him to ask you or because you don't want him to ask you?" Cozy asked—even though she already knew the answer.

"You dork! You know I'm totally in love with Dylan Hill," Ashley giggled.

Cozy smiled. "I know you are, and I'm sure he'll ask you…especially if you wear my pink sweater. It's my good luck sweater."

"I know, huh?" Ashley giggled. "Thanks, Cozy," she said.

"You're welcome," Cozy laughed. "Now close the door. I've got the breakfast shift again tomorrow."

"Okay. Love you."

"Love you too, Ash."

Ashley closed the door, and Cozy sighed. Setting her journal and pen on the nightstand, she turned off her reading lamp.

"Wonderful," she whispered, punching her pillow. "My sixteen-year-old sister and my *grandmother* have more exciting lives than I do."

Cozy closed her eyes and tried not to think of the mountain of ornaments she still needed to finish by the end of the week. She giggled then, however—smiled at the memory of the look of delight on her grandma's face when Cozy had suggested that Mr. Buckly Bryant might be a good kisser. It had been a precious expression—purely precious! As she struggled to settle all the thoughts bouncing around in her head, Cozy found herself wondering if her grandma's new neighbor really was a good kisser.

To the man of my dreams…
My husband, Kevin

ABOUT THE AUTHOR

Marcia Lynn McClure's intoxicating succession of novels, novellas, and e-books—including *Dusty Britches*, *The Whispered Kiss*, *The Haunting of Autumn Lake*, and *The Bewitching of Amoretta Ipswich*—has established her as one of the most favored and engaging authors of true romance. Her unprecedented forte in weaving captivating stories of western, medieval, regency, and contemporary amour void of brusque intimacy has earned her the title "The Queen of Kissing."

Marcia, who was born in Albuquerque, New Mexico, has spent her life intrigued with people, history, love, and romance. A wife, mother, grandmother, family historian, poet, and author, Marcia Lynn McClure spins her tales of splendor for the sake of offering respite through the beauty, mirth, and delight of a worthwhile and wonderful story.

BIBLIOGRAPHY

A Bargained-For Bride
Beneath the Honeysuckle Vine
A Better Reason to Fall in Love
The Bewitching of Amoretta Ipswich
Born for Thorton's Sake
The Chimney Sweep Charm
A Crimson Frost
Daydreams
Desert Fire
Divine Deception
Dusty Britches
The Fragrance of her Name
A Good-Lookin' Man
The Haunting of Autumn Lake
The Heavenly Surrender
The Highwayman of Tanglewood
Kiss in the Dark
Kissing Cousins
The Light of the Lovers' Moon
Love Me
The Man of Her Dreams
The McCall Trilogy
Midnight Masquerade
An Old-Fashioned Romance
One Classic Latin Lover, Please
The Pirate Ruse
The Prairie Prince
The Rogue Knight
Romantic Vignettes
Saphyre Snow